REMEMBER THE NIGHT

Sally Falcon

A KISMET™ Romance

METEOR PUBLISHING CORPORATION
Bensalem, Pennsylvania

To Gina F. Wilkins, my technical advisor—
I still owe you 56 pages.

SALLY FALCON

An avid romance reader since junior high school, Sally didn't try her hand at writing until years later. While busy establishing herself as a librarian, she accepted a dare from a friend to write a romance. She likes to combine the mood of the romantic comedy films of the 1930's and 1940's with settings taken from the eight states where she's lived. Currently, she lives in Arkansas—a transplanted *Yankee*—juggling her two careers.

ONE

"Oh, sweet heaven, it can't be him." Joanna Trent squeezed her eyes shut and opened them again. He was still there. Ruthlessly she closed the back of her throat, trapping the hysterical scream that was forming before it could escape. *This can't be happening to me, not today.* Forgetting the petite silver-blond at her side—and everyone else in the crowded ballroom—Joanna watched with horrified fascination as the dark-haired man walked away from the door to join a cluster of people nearby.

"Jo, what is it? Do you feel all right?" Diane Barringer looked at her friend and business partner in confusion. A strangling noise sounded directly in her ear, and it came from Joanna, who suddenly seemed frozen in place, her green eyes fixed on a point across the room. There was a look of abject fear on her usually poised face. "What did Dr. Jessop say about your check-up today?"

"The man in the brown suit standing next to Evan Hartford, who is he?" Joanna asked abruptly. She forced the words between clenched teeth, so they came out in a whispered hiss instead of her usual husky tone. There wasn't time to worry about her health right now.

Diane turned her head, then gave a short laugh. It was

easy to locate the commanding gray-haired figure of the president of Hartford Consolidated—and host of the reception that Trent-Barringer had organized. A tall, dark-haired man in his early thirties stood next to him. "Relax, it's his nephew. I met him while you were out with the flu, just before you went to Nassau."

Nassau. The word sent a shiver of emotion skating up Joanna's spine. Ruthlessly suppressing the bone-melting image it brought to mind, she grasped her friend's arm, unconsciously exerting pressure with her tapered fingernails. "His name, what's his name?"

"Hey, take it easy. That's Nathan Hartford. Don't worry though, he's harmless. Tanned, gorgeous, and with the sexiest mustache I've ever seen, but harmless to our public relations business," Diane replied with another slight laugh, but she gave Joanna a curious look when she made another strange noise.

"That's what you think," Joanna replied, taking pride in her normal sounding voice. She'd managed to keep the scream at bay, but she wasn't sure for how long. "Diane, I'll be right back. I'm going to the ladies."

She turned and walked briskly away before Diane could ask any awkward questions, or her nervous stomach could embarrass her in front of a room full of strangers. As she skirted the side of the ballroom, she kept a wary eye on both the Hartford men. Nathan hadn't seen her, yet. She had to do some fast thinking before he did. He was smiling that heart stopping, slanted grin; she wondered what would happen to that grin if she told him about the phone call this afternoon.

Would he be as devastated as she had been? No, that was undoubtedly wishful thinking. She was nothing more than a pleasant holiday diversion to him, not someone who had haunted his dreams for the past two months. It was possible that he didn't remember her at all.

Potent danger. Joanna recalled the words that blazed across her mind the moment she'd first laid eyes on Nathan two months ago. She'd been napping on the float in the middle of the cove and opened her eyes to discover—

Shaking her head, she dismissed the tantalizing memory of his smoky gray eyes watching her with amused speculation.

She slapped her hand harder than necessary against the swinging door of the restroom. The lounge area was deserted. Her nausea had passed for now, and she sank gratefully onto the nearest mauve brocade vanity bench. Burying her face in her hands, she muttered dark invectives at herself, Nathan, the entire world. The day began a slow descent toward disaster with an innocent phone call, and now was close to rock bottom at Nathan's sudden appearance.

How many times have I wondered about his last name in the past two months? She answered the question with another groan. Looking into the wall length mirror, she knew her carefully arranged French plait should be stark white instead of brunette with reddish-blond highlights. Shock was supposed to do that. She'd classify the whole day as a shocker of the horror variety, *Friday the Thirteenth,* parts one through one hundred and ninety-nine.

"*You* decided after twenty-nine and a half years that you were tired of being too practical, too level-headed, and too responsible. *You* had to be carefree and spontaneous, didn't you?" She challenged her oval faced reflection, noting the paleness of her skin. It wasn't just the loss of her holiday tan. "*You* had to prove *that* by having a whirlwind, no-holds-barred holiday affair with a man whose last name you didn't even know. The same man who just walked in the ballroom, and judging from his last name, is one of the new owners of the company that's your biggest client."

The whoosh of the outer door stopped Joanna's almost hysterical monologue. She sighed in relief that the woman entering wasn't from the Hartford party. Taking a deep breath, she knew she couldn't hide in the restroom all evening. The situation wouldn't change. Nathan would still be there whenever she returned to the party. With one last pleading look in the mirror she stood up, not bothering to correct the dejected angle of her shoulders as she walked to the door.

Though she knew she had to face him, Joanna wasn't prepared for the male figure leaning against the wall, not four feet from the door. In spite of her recent lecture, her knees suddenly had the consistency of cooked spaghetti. It was so tempting to go back inside—forever. Nathan straightened his six foot, two inch frame from his negligent position and her mind whirled, trying to think of something, anything to say.

The man was a walking, breathing fantasy from the top of his thick brown hair to the tips of his Italian leather shoes. She knew that his blatant sensuality was only muted by the European-cut suit. It was intensified three hundred percent when he wore that excuse of black material he called swim trunks—or when he wore nothing at all. Joanna was tempted to caress the lean plane of his cheek before his heated gaze turned from polished onyx to an icy gray when she told him—

Nathan took control, silently drawing her into his arms. While he nibbled on her lower lip, Joanna had one thought. *Maybe I'm panicking for nothing. I don't have to tell him anything until I'm sure.* Then she gave herself up to the possession of his kiss. She'd allow herself this one, last kiss, surrendering to the sweet singing sensations in her bloodstream that returned the minute she saw him again.

Sanity returned when the door opened behind them,

allowing Joanna to breathe once more. Nathan smiled graciously at the woman's derisive look before she disappeared around the corner. The lady wasn't aware that Nathan bent to devote all his attention to the shell of Joanna's ear.

"Surprised?" His deep, licorice-laced voice breathed into the tender skin of her neck. Delicately tracing the outline of her ear with an inquisitive tongue, he waited for her reply. He raised his head, a frown furrowing his high forehead and drawing his straight brows together.

Joanna remained silent, staring helplessly into his perplexed face. She memorized every line of his handsome countenance, wishing she dared stroke his thick mustache once more, or trace the outline of his full lower lip one last time.

His endearing half smile that creased one cheek and cocked his soft mustache at an angle was almost tentative, making her heart skip a beat. The warmth of his eyes searched her face for an answer she couldn't, wouldn't give. Her breath caught in her throat at the feel of his large, powerful hands gliding over her sensitive rib cage. Closing her eyes for a second, she savored the sensation, trying to gather together the ragged pieces of her rational mind.

With precarious resolve, she smiled through trembling lips. Fleetingly she caressed his cheek, letting the words rush out before she gave into her treacherous thoughts. "I'm sorry. I can't talk right now, Nathan. There's too much to be done at the reception."

Spinning on her heel, she fled. As she hurried away, she blocked out the look of astonishment on his face. It had to be a trick of her imagination. Sophisticated men like Nathan didn't take holiday flings seriously. Dismissing the treacherous image, she focused on one thought. She needed more time to think.

"Strike three, old man," Nathan murmured, rubbing his hand against the tense muscles at the back of his neck. His frown deepened as he watched Joanna's willowy figure disappear around the corner. This was the third time she'd left him totally confused, first on the float, then suddenly leaving Nassau without a word, and now this.

He'd anticipated her surprise, but he hadn't expected her to run at the first sight of him. The eager expectancy that buoyed his spirits all day evaporated. Where was the enchanting smile, the sparkling almond shaped eyes smoldering with desire, Joanna's voice murmuring his name with that sexy little catch in it?

For the first time, he regretted taking Evan's advice to find the owner of Trent-Barringer during his business trip to Nassau. It hadn't been much of a hardship once he'd discovered Joanna Trent was the same leggy brunette he'd spotted crossing the hotel lobby wearing a hot pink tank top and running shorts. He set out to meet the lady incognito, planning to disclose their business connection later, much later.

Now he was back where he began that first day he'd struck out by coming on too strong. Joanna Trent was a lady who didn't respond to hyperactive hormones. No, he acknowledged, he'd regressed even farther back than that.

But why?

Joanna's green, gold-flecked eyes were now flat and lifeless. Her tawny, soft skin was pale, tautly stretched over her delicate bone structure, overemphasizing her classic cheek bones. Though her full, inviting lips responded to his kiss, her smile afterward had been hesitant, almost nervous. And the soft, shoulder length hair he'd threaded his fingers through was now tamed into an elegant upsweep.

The only part of Joanna that seemed the same was her tall, curved body, at least what he'd felt through the black dress that covered her from a cowl collar to her ankles. He allowed himself to think longingly of her yellow string bikini and her breath-catching blue halter dress that almost had a top.

Out of the corner of his eye, Nathan saw another woman turn into the hallway. Her apprehensive look reminded him where he was loitering. Giving her a sardonic glance that matched his mood, he started back to the Hartford reception for its newly acquired employees from the Tri-Tex merger. Nearing the ballroom, he hastily decided his next plan of action, one that would be more successful than Plan A. He'd find Joanna and make plans to meet later in the evening.

"So much for Plan B," Nathan muttered under his breath a half hour later. Joanna was circulating and talking to everyone in the room, except him. Every time he discovered her new location, she'd disappear seconds later. Tired of this wild goose chase, he knew it was time for Plan C, reinforcements.

"Nat, my boy, you're just in time," came his uncle's jocular greeting from a group of employees. "We were about to toast the company."

"To Hartford Consolidated," the group saluted in unison, but Nathan's attention was on a cluster of people a few feet away. His hand clenched around the highball glass that was thrust into his hand. The man standing next to Joanna had his arm around her. He couldn't quite define the feeling that shot through his body. It was almost like a fist connecting unexpectedly with his solar plexus. Slowly the effect began to fade and anger overcame all other thoughts. He kept himself in tight control.

"Evan, I haven't met George Collins yet. Where is our fair haired boy?" Nathan ignored his uncle's surprised look at his curt tone. He kept his eyes pinned on George Collins, the man with his arm around Joanna.

"Well, follow me, son," Evan answered without hesitation, "we'll take care of that little detail right now."

Nathan walked silently next to the older man. He sized up Collins within a few seconds, an ingrained habit. He knew the man was brilliant from his personnel records; however, the file only gave statistics and job performance. It didn't mention the slender man wore one green and one rust colored sock with a navy suit, or the dollop of chip dip on his striped tie. This was the man he wanted to take apart limb by limb for touching Joanna.

As he moved closer Nathan dismissed Collins from his mind, focusing all his attention on Joanna. He narrowed his gaze. She stiffened suddenly, though seemingly absorbed in the conversation with the small blond in the scarlet dress.

"George, you haven't met my nephew yet, and I think Joanna was on vacation during Nathan's last visit," Evan said in total innocence before handling the official introductions. "We'll get the formalities out of the way tonight. Trent-Barringer will be seeing a lot of Nathan over the next few weeks while we get settled in St. Louis."

"Oh, how nice," Joanna responded politely, but Nathan knew her tone implied otherwise as he took her hand in a firm grip. The sable eyelashes that shielded her eyes flew upward the second he increased the pressure on her slender fingers.

"The pleasure will be all mine, believe me," he returned before releasing her hand. Looking deep into her wide-eyed green gaze, he was oblivious to their interested audience.

"Of course, she also seems to have a vested interest in Hartford Consolidated these days, not just our public relations contract," Evan continued, oblivious to the undercurrents in the small group. "George surprised us all when he walked in with this young lady on his arm tonight. He never mentioned that he'd been dating Joanna, the cagey devil."

Cagey, my foot. Joanna disciplined her features to remain passive. *He's up to something, but what I don't know.* She still hadn't recovered from her astonishment over George's announcement. As usual when George was attempting to deal with anything away from his work, he forgot a few minor details, like telling her what he was doing. What would he have done if she'd had a date with her?

"Indeed." Nathan said the single word with great deliberation, making Joanna wonder if she'd spoken out loud. Then she realized he was simply answering his uncle.

"Will you excuse us?" Diane stepped in before the uncomfortable silence could continue. "I see one of the waiters signaling to us. I'm sure we'll see you later, now that the dancing's started."

Joanna allowed her friend—and savior—to grab her limp arm and hurry her towards the buffet table. She waited silently while Diane made a show of consulting the surprised waiter with a few innocuous questions. Escape was Joanna's first thought, but she knew Diane would bombard her with questions about Nathan at any minute. The itching sensation between her shoulder blades told her that a certain pair of gray eyes were still watching her every move.

"Now, what was that all about?" Diane demanded without pausing to see if the waiter carried out her instructions.

"*That* was in Nassau two months ago," Joanna answered with false brightness, bracing herself for a barrage of questions. Diane's teasing speculation was much safer than

Nathan's sardonic look that didn't bode well for her, so she'd keep the mood light.

"Wow! You certainly kept that pretty quiet, hon," Diane exclaimed, accompanying it with a low whistle after glancing over her shoulder, "not that I blame you."

"There really wasn't anything to mention," Joanna explained with an airy wave of one hand. Diane's baby blue eyes were already wide with astonishment without any of the juicy details.

"Not much to mention, my foot. I saw the way he looked at you. If you met in Nassau, why did he need an introduction?"

"Because he only knew my first name and that I was recuperating from the flu," *and exactly where my birthmark is.* She gave the other woman a worldly smile, at least she hoped it was worldly. Diane's eyes widened still further and her mouth dropped open. "We agreed not to pry into each other's private lives, just vacation chitchat."

Diane swallowed with great deliberation, giving her blond curls a slight shake before letting an appreciative chuckle escape her lips. "I congratulate you on having excellent taste. I just hope George's little scheme doesn't aggravate Nathan too much. This is a gentleman you should keep around."

"What *was* that nonsense earlier?" Joanna asked, grasping at the change in subject and wondering why Diane blushed a cherry red that matched her dress. What did her best friend know about George?

"The rumor is that the Hartfords are looking for men with stable backgrounds for promotion," Diane answered, chewing on her lower lip as Joanna raised one eyebrow. "George is interested in a special project that's in the works. If he can show that he's developing a serious, respectable relationship, he thinks Evan will consider him for it.''

''Good old, idiotic George,'' his sister murmured without malice. So, George was confiding in Diane now, very interesting. ''Well, if we're lucky Evan will take his cue tonight and give George the project, and my dear brother won't bother with me again.''

''Nassau must have been interesting, if you're taking George's little trick this well. Wouldn't mind a little more vacation chit-chat with Nathan, hmmmm?'' Diane asked with a grin, wiggling her eyebrows, clearly recovering from her uncharacteristic display of shyness.

As usual Diane's sunny personality had Joanna back on track. At least with her friend's help, the situation didn't seem completely impossible. She'd simply overreacted. Nathan wasn't menacing, and Dr. Jessop had only been joking. Matching her friend's lighthearted attitude, she gave her an exaggerated leer, ''It *is* better in the Bahamas.''

''Now, come on, we'd better find my brother and drag him away from whatever technical discussion he's embroiled in,'' she continued, feeling better than she had all evening. She wasn't, however, going to take any unnecessary risks. ''If I'm his date, then he's going to play the attentive escort, whether he likes it or not.''

''If we're lucky he might even remember who we are,'' Diane added as they began their search.

''All right, children, put on your best party manners,'' Paul Stanley, Hartford Consolidated's personnel manager, announced to the others at the table. ''Here comes the boss.''

Joanna didn't have to turn her head to know it was Nathan, not Evan, heading their way. Her inner radar was finely tuned to his every move. For the past hour he'd been tormenting her from a distance, always watching.

Luckily, no one noticed how often her eyes were drawn to his quiet figure, or that her glance would barely meet his before skating away. A throbbing pain was building at the base of her neck.

"Paul, that's terrible. You act like Nathan's some kind of ogre." Diane's rebuke was softened by her teasing smile at the man who'd appointed himself as her escort the minute they met.

"Nothing of the sort. I just don't like the competition," Paul replied, brushing his finger playfully over her chin.

With Diane occupied with Paul, Joanna played idly with the ice cubes floating at the top of her club soda. Without looking up she knew the precise moment Nathan stopped beside the table. The dull pain in her head sharpened as he seemed to hover over the table like an avenging angel. She barely heard Nathan's coolly courteous voice asking George's permission to dance with her.

"Thank you, Mr. Hartford," Joanna answered before her brother could. Scarlett O'Hara would be proud of her simpering tone. "Please don't feel duty bound to dance with a business associate."

"My dear Ms. Trent, this isn't strictly a duty dance. Evan informed me that you're an excellent partner." His tone assured her he was remembering exactly how well they danced together. Her five foot eight inches complimented his own height perfectly.

"If you insist." She allowed him to pull her to her feet. His mood didn't permit an argument, and she knew he wouldn't hesitate to embarrass her. His mind was set on one purpose; unfortunately, she wasn't sure what it was.

They danced in silence for a few moments. Joanna braced herself expectantly. She wasn't aware of the speculative gleam in Nathan's eyes as he watched her averted face. When his voice sounded directly in her ear, she couldn't stop her start of surprise.

"I much prefer you without clothes.

"Ah, I thought that would get you to look at me," he said with satisfaction as she turned to look at him for the first time. "Of course, we must consider the change in climate. It's been slightly chilly in here all evening and you need to take care of those gorgeous shoulder blades. You'd be courting frost bite wearing that little blue number here instead of Nassau."

"I really can't see what concern my clothes could be to you," she said for lack of anything else to say.

"I'm not concerned about your clothing," he replied smoothly, his deep voice shivering down her spine. "It's the lack of it. I'm sure Collins would prefer the blue dress, too."

She didn't bother to answer, knowing the whole conversation was ridiculous. He seemed intent on making her lose her temper. If it was anyone else she would simply walk away, leaving him in the middle of a crowded dance floor. Since he was an important client and George's boss, she took refuge in silence.

"How could a spirited woman like you get involved with an eccentric character like Collins, a borderline geek?" he demanded hotly, going directly to the attack.

"What do you know—" Joanna broke off as he raised his eyebrows and pulled her even closer into his embrace. She couldn't very well challenge his ability to know what type of woman she was. He had an all too clear reason to think he knew without a doubt, unaware the Joanna in Nassau wasn't the same woman he was holding.

"I have known George quite a long time," she began again, *from the day he was born*. "We deal very well together. We always have."

"Oh, I'm sure you do," he said, his skepticism very apparent. "Is that why you were off in Nassau alone, very willing to pursue other interests?"

She was saved from answering as the music stopped. With a quick step she tried to elude his hands, but Nathan was too alert. His arms closed around her, pulling her against his hard frame as the band began playing once more. Joanna didn't want a confrontation, so she silently followed his lead. All she had to do was keep her mouth shut and get through the dance.

"I'll give you one week to get rid of Collins." Nathan almost hated himself for the threat, but he was desperate. He had to break through her icy facade.

Joanna looked up at him with a glare, then drew back when she realized how close he was. As he maneuvered them away from the other dancers, he watched her glance nervously to the side. What had gone wrong between them? She wasn't angry, so she didn't know about his little deception in Nassau. She was extremely uneasy, however. How serious was her relationship with Collins?

"I won't repeat that," he growled, maintaining his grim pose as his frustration began to escalate. He wanted his carefree, unpredictable Joanna back. The laughing woman who'd dared him to carry her into the bedroom of his suite without dropping her. "I'm also perfectly willing to make a scene unless we step into the service area behind us."

Joanna didn't argue. Without a word she stepped out of his arms and preceded him into the deserted room. It was apparent from the disorder that a waiter could return at any minute. Nathan knew he didn't have much time. When she whirled around to face him, he was ready. He took her in his arms, stopping her words with a fierce kiss. In his anger and frustration, he tried demanding a response, but Joanna remained passive.

He cautioned himself to move slower. Trailing his lips across her cheek to the soft skin below her ear, he couldn't stem his impatience. "You don't watch enough soap operas, love." He nipped her ear in chatisement before laving his tongue over the bite. "No resistance is more of an inducement than resistance to an angry man. Respond, then we'll talk."

He knew the demand was arrogant and chauvinistic, but he didn't give her time to reply. In place of his previous aggression, he teased her lips apart. The gentle caress succeeded in eliciting a small response that satisfied him.

"Kiss me, Joanna. Put your lovely arms around my neck and tangle your bewitching fingers in my hair, sweet nymph, or I swear I'll go into the ballroom and describe every minute of our time together over the microphone."

He went still, waiting. Was he wrong? Had the magic between them just been part of the tropical atmosphere? Slowly Joanna's arms encircled his neck; his heart beat accelerated as her tapered fingers wreaked havoc with his perfectly styled hair. Briefly her lips nibbled over the soft bristles of his mustache before she deepened the kiss. Nathan kept himself in rigid control, reveling in her touch. He hadn't dreamed this. She stroked the inner warmth of his mouth. Every motion was what he'd dreamed about since he'd woken in Nassau to find her gone.

He couldn't remain passive to the exquisite torture a minute longer. Joanna shivered when his hands moved lightly over the smooth line of her back. Nathan wanted to shout for joy. He'd broken through her icy disdain. This was his Joanna. He was impatient to dismiss Collins from her life and return to what they began in Nassau, but he couldn't let her go right now.

Unable to resist, he reached upward to cup her full breasts. Joanna's hips moved impatiently against his swollen need in answer to the gentle pressure. It only whetted his appetite for more intimacy, and they were in the wrong place.

"Oh, Lord, Joanna. I wanted you to respond, not half kill me." He pressed his mouth against the wildly beating pulse at the base of her throat, hoarsely murmuring the words into her heated skin.

His impassioned words hit Joanna like an icy wave of water, bringing her back to her senses. She lunged away from Nathan, horrified at what she'd just done. All he had to do was touch her, and she forgot everything that mattered—her job, her brother, her sanity. She tried to think how she should react as the haze of her arousal began to clear.

Nathan moved toward her, a perplexed look on his face, and she stepped back, holding her hand in front of her to ward off his touch. She knew that guilt and self-righteous indignation were needed, but rational thoughts were being clouded by despair. She had to recoil from Nathan when all she wanted was to return to his arms. But that was the worst thing she could do under the circumstances.

"You egotistical, arrogant—" she faltered as she remembered the precarious situation. This man was a client, as well as her lover in Nassau. With as much dignity as she could muster, she drew herself up, controlling her erratic breathing. "Mr. Hartford, I'll ignore this incident and the rest of this evening." She forced her voice to drip with disdain as she gave him a scathing look. "We had a good time in Nassau, but that was two months ago. It was a pleasant interlude I plan to forget. Excuse me."

She left the small room without a backward glance, missing the dejected slump of Nathan's shoulders. She swept passed the inquisitive waiter she encountered two steps from the doorway, her eyes on Diane and George. All she thought about was escaping. She had to put some distance between Nathan and herself. Too much had happened today, and she had to think about what to do. Before she did anything else, she had to consider what Dr. Jessop said over the phone this afternoon.

In a manner of minutes, she convinced the others that

she needed to leave due to a blinding headache. With Diane's eager assistance, she managed to pry George loose to drive her home. The drive was quiet. George was lost in his own world as usual; Joanna was trying to erase everything from her mind. After a stop at the drug store, they headed for her apartment.

"George, what possessed you to tell Evan Hartford I was your girlfriend?" she asked, cutting through the silence of the dark car as he turned into the parking lot. She knew she should be used to her brother's starts by now, but he always managed to surprise her. "I'm beginning to wish—not for the first time—we'd been adopted by total strangers instead of sisters. I'd be an only child, without an idiot for a brother."

"But then I couldn't have said you were my girlfriend," George answered, totally missing Joanna's point. His one track mind was working on his own problem. "When Hartford began questioning me about my social life, I thought about all those times you helped with my girlfriends. You know, pretending to be the other woman when they started making marriage noises. You were the perfect one to help me make a good impression on Hartford. Our last names are different, and you wouldn't make trouble later."

It made perfect sense, unfortunately, and she really was more than partially to blame. She'd been overly protective of her younger brother since their natural parents were killed in a car accident when she was six and George was four. They hadn't been separated when they'd been fortunate at the unlikely ages of ten and eight to be adopted. Amanda Trent and Theresa Collins were sisters, who had contacted the orphanage at the same time. Though neither the Trents nor the Collins could take both children, they'd quickly made preparations to keep the small family intact. In spite of the security of two loving families, George continued to turn to Joanna for guidance and occasional rescue. And old habits die hard, she decided fatalistically.

"You should have told me before the reception," Joanna explained very slowly, hoping the words would sink into his thick head. "I would like to have been prepared for it."

"I forgot."

Joanna sank lower in the car seat while George parked the car. She should have known that was what happened. There wasn't a mean bone in George's body or an ounce of guile, unless it came to his ditsy girlfriends. The man needed a keeper, but she was tired of being elected. Rashly she decided to try reversing their roles for a change.

"George, I met Nathan Hartford when I was in Nassau."

"And?" her brother returned, seeming to realize there was some significance in her statement.

Looking at his wide-eyed turquoise gaze, masked slightly by his oversized glasses, Joanna sighed with regret and gathered up her purse and the sack from the drug store. "Never mind, dear. Good night."

"You didn't get in over your head, did you?"

His question froze her hand on the door handle. She should have known better. Once George gave his attention to something, he would stick to it. The only thing he showed an aptitude for besides his work was sex. "No, of course not. We met briefly, we didn't even exchange last names."

"No last names? And I always thought you were fairly respectable." George gave a shout of laughter. "Do you always pick up strange men on vacation?"

"Oh, really, George. It wasn't like that at all," Joanna lied, annoyed at his teasing. She thought he might be anxious about this new complication, instead he was making fun of her. He never did what was expected. "If that's the way you're going to be, I'm going inside."

She scrambled out of the car and slammed the door. His teasing rankled even more than Diane's surprise earlier. Did everyone always expect her to be so rigidly responsible? George's laughter mocked her as she ran up the walk, but she wasn't fast enough to outdistance him. He caught her at the entrance.

"Jo, I know it wasn't anything like that. Most of your dates are lucky to get a handshake," he reassured her, not realizing he was making her feel worse. "It's just that you don't get into something you can't handle very often. I'm glad to see you're human."

"May the Lord save me from smug relatives." She had a juvenile urge to kick him in the shins. It seemed everyone but Joanna was allowed to have fun. Good, old, dull, practical Joanna wasn't supposed to behave like a normal woman. Was it any wonder she'd done something crazy on her first vacation in years? It wasn't any comfort that she was paying for it now.

"Now, Jo," George began rather pompously, then started laughing again. "I'd love to have been there to see you matching wits with a professional bachelor like Nathan. He must be quite a handful."

"I can see you aren't taking this seriously. It could be bad for Trent-Barringer as well as for you," she shot back, more than tempted to tell him exactly what had happened in Nassau, and afterwards. With one look at the smirk on his face, she gave up. "We'll talk about this some other time."

"All right, we'll sleep on it, but don't get too worked up," he responded, finally containing his amusement. "It won't threaten your precious business. Nathan knows the rules, and would be the last person to let a little vacation romance interfer with business. He was probably a little put out tonight that an attractive lady was suddenly out of reach. Tomorrow he'll have forgotten all about it.''

''You're probably right,'' she said with a sigh, knowing that he was. Why didn't she find any comfort in his reassurances? Absently kissing her brother good night, she went inside, wishing she possessed his singlemindedness. Unfortunately, the sack she clutched in her hand was a reminder of the problem of Nathan Hartford.

The next morning as she paced the living room, Joanna finally had the blinding headache that excused her from the Hartford reception. A stress filled evening and a sleepless night were undoubtedly the cause. What was she going to do? When Dr. Jessop called yesterday about the results of her check-up, she'd experienced mild panic at his teasing words, then dismissed the idea as stress related. However, that was before Nathan appeared. Panic couldn't describe what she felt now.

Looking down the hallway toward the bathroom as if waiting for Freddy Krueger to appear, she remembered exactly what Dr. Jessop had said. ''The tests were all fine. You're probably just pushing yourself too hard as usual. It certainly isn't that flu bug that got you a few months ago. In fact, if I didn't know better, I'd think you might be pregnant.''

Well, she knew better. Even if she wanted to deny it, she couldn't. There was a little plastic stick lying on the bathroom sink, one end of it blazing a bright blue. Nathan Hartford didn't know it, but he was going to be a father in about seven months, damn it.

TWO

"You look like you slept on a bed of nails last night," Diane commented as Joanna groped her way into the car.

"Who slept?" Joanna complained, then leaned her head back carefully against the head rest. She closed her eyes to shut out the bright, early morning sunshine. Her body was still trying to recover from terminal morning sickness that made her pregnancy test almost redundant. After an hour her stomach finally settled down, but she felt like a wrung out dishrag.

"Nightmares?"

Joanna recognized that deceptively light tone of voice. She knew without opening her eyes that Diane had a thousand questions on the tip of her tongue. They'd set the pattern during their four year partnership. No matter how tantalizing or intriguing, each would wait until the other was ready to talk. Diane's blue eyes were undoubtedly wide with anticipation while she nibbled on her lower lip.

"One big nightmare—Nathan Hartford. I spent most of the night trying to figure out how to avoid him and still keep the Hartford account," Joanna grumbled, wondering how and when to tell Diane the truth. She turned her head to regard her friend through one eye. Diane was gnawing on her lip as she drove down Clayton Road at a steady rate. Now wasn't the right time. "I've settled on murder, but can't quite come up with the best candidate, Nathan or George, who's running a close second."

Diane gave a musical laugh as she always did when Joanna threatened her brother with grievous bodily harm. Then her expression became serious, and she glanced briefly away from the morning traffic. "If I'd known what George was planning last night, I'd have been glad to volunteer."

"That's very noble of you, but—" The look on Diane's face finally made an impact on Joanna's tired brain, and she opened both eyes to study the blond's profile. Diane had the same militant look on her pixish face as the day she'd walked into Trent Enterprises four years ago, telling an overworked Joanna that her company was in desperate need of Diane's artistic talents.

"You'd better have some of that coffee I sacrificed life and limb for among the caffeine addicts at the convenience store," Diane instructed, nodding toward the Styrofoam cup in the holder under the dashboard.

Joanna sat up slowly—wishing she could be a morning person instead of a late afternoon type—and reached forward without taking her eyes off the other woman. Tomorrow she'd start adjusting her diet to her condition, but right now she needed coffee. Diane didn't say a word while Joanna gingerly removed the plastic lid and took a gratifying sip. Unfortunately, the steaming liquid didn't clear the cotton wool from her brain. She wasn't in any shape for a real life conversation at this time of day and proved it by asking, "Diane, are you putting me on? George?"

"Well, why not? Someone needs to take care of him during his lapses from rational thought." She glanced at her friend and gave a philosophical shrug. "I have an overactive maternal streak, I guess."

Joanna was stunned. She always thought Diane looked on her brother as a nuisance. Though she loved George dearly, she also knew Diane Barringer had very few weekends without dates. Standing barely five feet and weighing just over ninety pounds with the help of heavy clothing, Diane was always in demand. A feathery cap of silver blond curls framing a heart-shaped face with a small, slightly turned up nose and enormous sky blue eyes seemed to bring out the male protective instinct. One man went so far as calling her his pocket goddess. Joanna sometimes envied Diane's petite figure. At times her own height made her imagine herself a towering Amazon with a cherub in tow.

The more she considered her brother and Diane, however, the more ideal it sounded. Besides, Diane would also make a terrific aunt. She was surprised she hadn't thought of it herself. Unfortunately, George's taste in women ran to extremely flashy looks with I.Q.s of frozen shrimp.

"You're awfully quiet. Did I say something wrong?" Diane asked in a tentative voice as she braked behind a line of cars at a four-way stop. She turned to face Joanna, a hesitant expression on her face.

"Absolutely not," Joanna hurried to reassure her friend. "I think it's wonderful. The only problem is getting George's mind off his work and his floozies long enough to get the right idea. Of course, his little trick last night might just be his downfall."

"What do you mean?" Diane couldn't mask her eagerness, forgetting where they were until an impatient driver honked behind them.

"He says the Hartfords are looking for men with stable lives for their promotion ladder, right? You're very stable and his sister's closest friend," Joanna explained while Diane inched the car forward. "I think George needs more attention from his sister and her closest friend right now. Let proximity and maybe a little female ingenuity do its magic."

"Fine, we'll forget all about the Hartfords and work on George instead," Diane agreed and laughed as she accelerated through the intersection.

Joanna glanced at the plum silk suit that hugged Diane's trim figure and grinned. "If you keep wearing ammunition like that suit, or the red dress you wore last night, George won't know what hit him."

With that piece of advice, Joanna leaned back for a short catnap for the rest of the drive. At least that's what she wanted Diane to think. She had a lot of decisions to make about her pregnancy, especially if she was going to tell Nathan. There wasn't any question that she would have the baby and raise it herself. Though she'd been a happily adopted child, she wouldn't consider giving the baby away. But how would Nathan feel about it?

She had plenty of time to make a decision. Concentrating on her business would be the perfect way to avoid thinking about Nathan for the time being. Seeing him in her dreams was enough. She knew she would have to face him with the truth soon, but for now, she could play ostrich and lose herself in her work. Her schedule would have to be adjusted for pregnancy leave and for after the baby arrived.

Trent-Barringer Enterprises was her own creation. When Alfred Trent died shortly after she got her MBA, Joanna stepped into his public relations business in an attempt to hold it together for her mother. The final year of his life had entailed a long illness after an inoperable brain tumor was diagnosed. By working doggedly the first year, Joanna had been able to salvage most of the major accounts. Then she began restructuring the business the second year when Diane approached her for a job.

Together they tailored the firm to cater to the needs of independent businesses who wanted to channel their time and manpower into their products and leave the task of promotion and entertainment in other hands. Diane headed the art department while Joanna handled the finances and client contacts. In four years the two women and their small, but select staff, had molded a respected and award winning company.

Joanna greeted her secretary in good humor when she entered the outer office with its soothing earth tone decor. She'd handled difficult problems in the past, and she could deal with the new twists in her life with the same positive approach. "Well, Anita, what's on hand for today?"

"Morning, Jo, Diane," returned the frosted haired woman in her early fifties, giving the two women her placid Mona Lisa smile. "The phone hasn't stopped ringing since I arrived, and the calls are all for Joanna."

"Oh, the price of popularity." Joanna let out an exaggerated languid sigh. "I don't know how you survived while I was out sick and then soaking up the rays in the Bahamas to regain my strength."

Diane looked up from a cup of tea at the white pine credenza behind Anita. "Very simple, my dear, we just told everyone we couldn't be bothered and to call back when you returned. Meanwhile, Anita and I played gin rummy and ate bon-bons to our hearts' content, just like we do every day."

"Cute," Joanna returned, knowing that Diane had efficiently performed as art director and handled Joanna's duties during the month that she'd been gone. She hadn't complained and had vehemently agreed when the doctor insisted that Joanna take her first vacation in years to avoid a relapse. Joanna was about to express her gratitude once again when Nathan's name seemed to jump out at her from the pink slip of paper in her hand.

"Joanna, are you all right? Your face has turned almost the same tomato red as your dress. Just what did Dr. Jessop say yesterday?" Diane asked without pausing for breath.

Joanna quickly looked down at the message and her breathing started again. "I'm fine, now that I realize Nathan isn't coming in this morning as scheduled. That will teach me to get lazy and not check my appointments a day ahead."

"Both Mr. Hartfords left messages this morning. Mr. Nathan Hartford was unexpectedly called to Chicago about a shopping center project," Anita supplied with her perfect recall that made her invaluable to Trent-Barringer. "Mr. Evan Hartford would like you to meet him for lunch at one o'clock. Oh, and the Kirkwood police called. George forgot his car at the grocery store again. The Schnucks manager notified them, so Sergeant Muldoon promised to park it in the driveway as usual, in case your brother remembers it's missing."

"Thank God he's in a car pool now, or he'd never get to work. I wonder what he did with my car last night," Joanna said with a resigned sigh. She wouldn't have any trouble raising a child after all her practice with George. She looked over at her partner who was calmly sipping her tea and gave Diane a sympathetic smile. "I hope you know what you're getting yourself into."

A few hours later Joanna remembered those words and wished she knew what *she* was doing as she got off the elevator at the Clayton Inn. Evan Hartford's secretary hadn't mentioned why he wanted this lunch meeting. Most of the morning she'd been distracted by her work, but during the last hour, she gave up altogether. An hour of pacing and wishing for the caffeine she couldn't have hadn't helped. She hadn't the faintest idea what Evan Hartford wanted.

Did he know about Nassau, or that George was really her brother, or was she just a paranoid idiot? She didn't have time to speculate further since Evan was standing at the hostess station. His tall, stiffly erect figure stood out among the others waiting to be seated.

"Ah, Joanna, here you are," Evan's deep voice boomed the minute he turned his head and spied her red clad figure. He gave her a welcoming smile that lit up his craggy face. "Luckily, I made a reservation, so we can get a table immediately."

She walked ahead of him to a table at the window, containing her nervousness. Her gray-haired companion was the same affable man from last night. However, he was a successful businessman, who could be hiding his knowledge behind a genial facade, just as she was taking refuge behind her professional mask.

"This is a very pleasant change from a room full of shirt sleeved engineers and stale sandwiches for the last few weeks," he announced when the waitress left them with their menus. He waved his hand toward the city that stretched out below them. "I can't say I was disappointed Nathan was called to Chicago, allowing me this opportunity. He was looking forward to seeing you again, however. You made quite an impression on the boy."

"How flattering," Joanna answered, hoping against hope her skepticism wasn't apparent. She smiled pleasantly while an entire herd of butterflies performed some ancient war dance in her stomach. "Boy" was hardly the word to describe Nathan.

"Actually, I'm giving you the wrong impression. Our meeting isn't about our account with Trent-Barringer." Evan gave her an apologetic smile that Joanna thought was a secret signal to the butterflies. Their wings grew longer, and they increased their rapid pace. "I lured you here under false pretenses. I wanted to talk about you."

"About me?" She had to wait for whatever he had in mind while the waitress took her order. Evan must know about Nassau, but it wasn't humanly possible for him to know that she was pregnant.

"I like to get to know the people I work with personally. It seems to make business go more smoothly," Evan continued once the waitress had disappeared. "I would have done this sooner, but Nathan's been traveling more than usual over the last few months. With him out of the office, I've been snowed under."

"I like your style, Evan," Joanna said, her voice even and controlled. She took a deep swallow of water to contain the whoop of relief that was clamoring to break out. "It's too bad more of my clients don't have the same philosophy."

"Thank you, my dear. Things have settled down a bit, so except for this emergency in Chicago, Nathan should be back in harness again to help with the administrative work here in St. Louis."

Joanna sat forward abruptly, the butterflies going into double time once more. "Nathan will be working in St. Louis? I didn't realize he was an active part of management. Diane's been handling the initial part of the change from Tri-Tex to Hartford Consolidated."

"Nathan's my right hand man as well as a top flight engineer. He'll take over the entire operation when I retire," Evan stated, his pride clear on his face. "Of course, his father wanted him to study law and join his practice in Philadelphia, but I'm glad he didn't. Just this morning he came up with a new approach to a job in Washington state. We're sending your friend Collins out there to get things started."

"I see," she replied for lack of anything to say. Was

it a coincidence that George was being sent halfway across the country? She really didn't want to know the answer. "When will George be leaving?"

"Tonight, I'm afraid. If we can get things cleared away this afternoon," he explained with an apologetic smile as the waitress set down their plates. "We decided the sooner the better. If the problem in Chicago hadn't developed, Nathan might have gone to take care of the preliminaries himself."

"Well, here's to George's success," Joanna toasted, raising her ice tea glass, amazed at the steadiness of her hand. *And to anything that keeps Nathan out of town.*

"I must compliment you on a very impressive, and innovative business, Joanna. You've added a unique touch to public relations with very happy results for your clients."

Joanna launched into an explanation of how she got started, her appetite suddenly returning now that they were on safe ground. Evan was a charming companion, and she was looking forward to working with him. From business, they progressed to their respective families.

"Your mother's lucky you're fairly close," Evan said in a wistful tone. "My girls are spread out. Elizabeth's in Alaska with her husband and Evelyn is on the west coast, so Alicia is the only one who's near us. Nathan's mother is always on me about sending him all over the country for weeks at a time. I guess I really can't complain."

"He seems to be pretty busy now," Joanna mumbled into her water glass, reluctant to return to the subject of his nephew.

"Yes, with this expansion only one of us could travel and Nathan was elected," his uncle acknowledged, pausing to give the waitress his credit card. "The poor boy hasn't gotten much rest over the last few months. First, he was in Savannah to look over a completed office building, then Chicago repeatedly on this shopping center and Nassau for a hotel complex. Not that a trip there was a real hardship.''

Joanna remained silent while Evan signed his credit receipt. They were back on thin ice suddenly, and she felt as though a large crack was materializing at her feet. The butterflies were replaced by a herd of rogue elephants. She wasn't sure where the conversation would lead, so she played dumb.

''You know it was a shame Nathan couldn't locate you when he was in Nassau,'' Evan commented once the waitress left. ''He needs someone like you. However, his loss is Collins's gain.''

''What?'' Joanna knew her voice was at a hysterical pitch, but she couldn't stop herself. Evan's words jolted her like an electric shock. Underlying her sudden anger a hurt voice was chanting a refrain: *Nathan knew. Nathan knew.*

''I guess I should apologize for being impertinent. My wife Helen is a compulsive matchmaker and her ideas must be rubbing off on me,'' he answered, seemingly unaware of her panic. ''She's been trying for years to get him to settle down. I'd heard so much about you from the Tri-Tex people, I didn't think it would hurt for Nathan to meet you before you began working together on our account.''

Joanna wanted to throw something or break something, and it frightened her. She'd never felt this kind of violent anger before in her life. If Nathan was there, she'd be wrapping her fingers around his throat. He'd known the entire time they were in Nassau exactly who she was. Until now she'd given him the benefit of the doubt. Now his uncle's innocent words condemned him as a liar and worse, a man with no feelings for anyone but himself. She knew the type all too well from experience.

Twisting her linen napkin tightly in her hands, she managed to control herself enough to hold a rational conversation. "Yes, it's a shame, but I don't think Nathan and I are really compatible."

"That's a pity," Evan replied and stood up as Joanna did. "I would like you to meet my wife when she visits next week, if that's convenient?"

"That would be lovely," she answered absently. She was amazed to discover that her unsteady legs were able to carry her out of the restaurant. She chatted with Evan on the trip down the elevator, and kept up her polite facade until they parted company on the sidewalk.

Her long legs ate up the few blocks of pavement on her way back to the office. Nathan Hartford was the most despicable man she'd ever met. He was going to pay for making a fool out of her. There wasn't any way in hell she was going to tell him about the baby now. Though she regretted lying to a nice man like Evan, Nathan didn't deserve to know the truth.

She wouldn't be side tracked any longer by the memory of his gray eyes deepening to black when he was about to kiss her. Nor would she remember the delicious feel of his large, callused hands caressing her skin. His deep voiced words of passion had all been a pose, part of his life. Like a naive school girl, she'd believed the impassioned whispers of a practiced man who had no feelings. She'd show Nathan that two could play the game of lying to gain their own end.

"You look like you're about to commit murder," Diane commented the second Joanna stepped through the glass and chrome door of Trent-Barringer's outer office. The words startled Joanna out of her dark thoughts.

"You told me that Nathan Hartford was harmless," she spat out, hurrying passed her astonished partner on her way into her office. She didn't bother to see if Diane followed, knowing the petite blond would be at her heels. Dropping into the tweed chair behind her desk, she glared at the other woman who slipped into the visitor's chair on the other side of the polished walnut surface.

"Not only is Nathan sending George to the Pacific coast on some cockamamie project, he knew who I was when we met in Nassau. His uncle told him to look me up."

"Holy cripe," Diane exclaimed, her eyes widening in amazement. "You haven't been this angry since that South American exec from Johnson Textiles made a pass at you, then had the nerve to propose as an apology."

"I'm madder," Joanna forced out between clenched teeth, drumming her fingers in a heavy tattoo against the desk blotter. "That man purposely set out to seduce me and now—" This still wasn't the time to talk about the baby.

She looked at her friend and wished she hadn't. Diane's expression was anxious, her eyes imploring her to talk about what happened with Nathan. Joanna, however, wasn't quite prepared to divulge just how foolishly she'd behaved and the result. Though Diane teased her about her strong sense of responsibility and her protectiveness of George, she wouldn't understand what had happened in Nassau. She wouldn't understand the sudden need Joanna felt to break out, rebel against years of common sense and self discipline.

Diane knew that Joanna grew up fast when her natural parents were killed in a car accident and that she'd looked out for George until they'd been adopted. What Diane couldn't possibly understand was the frivolous, devil-may-care spirit that overcame Joanna the first time she opened her eyes and met the sexy, slanted grin of Nathan Hartford that afternoon in the tropics. In fact, Joanna wasn't sure she understood it herself. It happened, but she'd picked a heartless rogue for her declaration of independence. She wasn't quite ready to announce her stupidity to the world, or even to her closest friend, not yet.

"I suppose I should be grateful since George is out from under foot for a while." Joanna forced herself to smile, hoping Diane would take the cue that she wasn't ready to talk.

Diane sighed, signaling her momentary defeat. "But why bother to send George out of town if Nathan's in Chicago?"

"The man isn't infallible," she answered with a grimace at the irony of her statement. Apparently that's how she'd gotten pregnant, one of his weaker moments. "I must say it will be convenient, now I can get a peaceful week of sleep without worrying about tripping over Nathan or worrying about George."

"Don't count on it. I don't think Nathan intends to be forgotten that easily." Diane's dry tone cut into Joanna's pleasant thoughts.

"What makes you say that?" She gave her partner a wary look through narrowed eyes.

"This arrived right after you left for lunch." *This* was a florist box that Diane pushed across the top of the desk. In her anger, Joanna hadn't noticed the white box with the cellophane window.

For a minute, she sat staring at the box as if it would explode. The temptation to dump it into the trash unopened was great, but her curiosity overcame the impulse. Inside was a single perfect orchid, a twin to the silk flower Joanna wore in her hair in Nassau, and left behind in Nathan's suite. Her name was written across the attached card in a bold scrawl. Gingerly she opened the envelope, chaffing at her own weakness.

I'll allow you a reprieve, but remember me on those cold, lonely nights while I'm gone. N.

"This guy is dynamite," Diane exclaimed with a whistle of appreciation.

Joanna looked up from the small white square, unaware that she'd read the message aloud. "This guy is pond scum. He's only playing a game to overcome his wounded male dignity. I'm the one that got away."

"I wouldn't be too hasty in second guessing his motives," Diane argued with her usual habit of seeing good in everyone. "That wasn't the look of a wounded man last night, more like a hungry tiger."

"Well, one of us losing sleep over it is enough," Joanna quickly replied, squelching an inner voice that wanted to agree, though she knew better. "I'll worry about Nathan when he gets back. Meanwhile, you need to concentrate on how to drag George's attention away from his drawing board and building designs."

"I'll let you get away with this for now," Diane warned, "but don't expect to keep me from asking how you're sleeping this week."

To Joanna's surprise, she barely had a moment to spare thinking about Nathan during the next week. Diane was right, however. She didn't sleep soundly—but she attributed that to her pregnancy and stress. Anita came down with a spring cold—becoming more hindrance than help as she tried to stay on the job—then, Joanna's assistant, Fred Simpson, broke his collar bone tripping over one of his son's roller skates. With Fred temporarily out of commission, Joanna was loaded down with work at the office and at home.

Her energy would lag about four o'clock every afternoon and she'd nap as soon as she got home. By bed time her over stimulated mind kept her awake, not the fact that each passing day brought Nathan's return closer. On Saturday Joanna was ready for a relaxing day at home, doing absolutely nothing. Unfortunately, she was too edgy to remain idle for the relaxing reading that she'd promised herself.

Finally, she decided to wear down her extra adrenaline with house cleaning; though she usually despised it, it would help keep her mind off Nathan. Despite her loathing for the man, she found herself falling into the trap of remembering whenever she had a quiet moment. The memories were bittersweet. Nathan as she'd first seen him on the float. The two of them alone, separated from the other sun worshipers. Nathan holding her on the dance floor, his tall, lean frame fitting perfectly with hers, whispering his own personal endearments in her ear. His subtle seduction in his suite and the dangerous memory of his lovemaking.

By noon she'd worked her way through the bedrooms, kitchen, and bathrooms. Then she got the urge to rearrange the living room, but once every piece of furniture was dragged to the center of the room her energy flagged. Stretching out on the sofa, she started to plan which room she'd turn into the nursery.

The sound of the door bell jarred her awake. For a moment she was slightly disoriented. Glancing at the clock she realized she'd been asleep for about a half hour. Then the bell chimed again. As nimbly as she could Joanna escaped the huddle of furniture. Whoever was there was impatient, a heavy finger holding down the button. If it was the paper boy he wasn't going to get a tip this month, no matter how appealing he tried to look.

"I'm here for heaven's sake, spare the innocent door bell," she cried cheerfully, yanking the door open. The sight of her visitor made her wish she'd never bothered.

"Very nice, but a little dramatic. A much better welcome than I expected," Nathan said, his tone amused from where he leaned casually against the wall.

Her first impulse was to slam the door in his face. She felt like a beggar in her dusty cut-offs and oversize chambray shirt as she took in his designer jeans and gold V-neck sweater. His sartorial image was completed by a plaid shirt of muted browns and blues that showed at his cuffs and neck. She was dressed for the taxing job of cleaning, while he was ready for the cool Missouri spring weather. Over the past week, she'd imagined countless situations for their next meeting, but none of them had her looking like a bare-footed ragamuffin with her hair in a pony tail.

He waited for her to finish her scrutiny, a grin creasing his face as each emotion registered on her face. "Is this as far as I get, or will you trust me inside?"

"No, but I suppose you'll come in anyway, invited or not," she answered. He confirmed her statement by walking past her without saying a word, pausing only for her to shut the door and point the way toward the living room.

"Make yourself at home," she offered with a small ounce of satisfaction at the room's disorder, waving a hand toward the shambles she'd made of the room.

"Where do you suggest I begin?" he asked, raising his straight brows in mild inquiry.

"You probably wouldn't like what I would suggest, so you can pull one of the chairs over near the fireplace." She wasn't pleased with herself for not leaving him on the other side of the closed door. While he occupied himself in shifting the chair, Joanna propped her shoulders against the mantel, crossing her fingers over her stomach in an absentmindedly protective gesture. When she realized what she'd done, she hastily crossed her arms over her unfettered breasts in what she hoped was a casual pose.

Nathan took an exaggerated amount of time settling into his chair, then studying the room's pleasing blend of powder blue, moss green, and egg shell white. When he finished, he regarded Joanna silently. She wouldn't give him the satisfaction of knowing how uncomfortable she felt under his lazy regard. Now she knew how a worm felt on a fish hook, but she was determined not to budge an inch, despite his smug expression.

"Can I get you something to drink?" she finally asked in desperation. His smoky stare was making her very aware she had nothing on under her shirt, wondering if he had guessed. She could barely keep from looking down to see if the knot under her breasts was still secure. Though there was a slight tenderness in her breasts, her stomach was still flat and smooth.

"No, thanks, I won't be staying that long." Just long enough to drive you stark, staring mad, his eyes seemed to add.

"Oh, really?" *I'll stay calm; I won't scream*, she repeated over and over to herself.

"We're long overdue for our talk, sweet nymph."

"There's nothing to discuss, Nathan," Joanna shot back, ignoring the fission of emotion that assailed her. It was a combination of fear and excitement. Fear that somehow he knew about the baby and aggravating excitement at the gravelly timbre of his voice caressing the special endearment. She tightened her arms against her breast as she continued to watch his smug expression. "I thought I made that clear last week."

His head tilted back to rest against the moss green upholstery of his chair. He watched her stiff figure from beneath his eyelashes and waited. Then his slow, slanted smile came into play, increasing her unease. "Oh, yes, that was quite a performance. I'm still not sure who it was for though. Was it for my benefit, or were you trying to convince yourself?"

"Let me know when you reach a conclusion." She knew her sarcasm was wasted on his Philadelphia Mainline arrogance, but she made the effort anyway. The man was incredible, though he'd hit fairly close to the truth. But he apparently didn't know about her enlightening conversation with his uncle. Since then, she hadn't had any trouble convincing herself that Nathan Hartford was a heartless swine.

"Don't worry, sweetheart, you'll be the first on my list," he returned, casually lifting his foot to rest his ankle on his thigh. He studied the toe of his loafer without bothering to look up. "Your week is up."

Joanna couldn't believe she heard the low tones correctly. He sat calmly inspecting his foot. All her apprehensions fled as her temper skyrocketed, and her common sense disappeared along with her fears about his visit. "Get out, get out right this minute." She advanced on him, ready to pull him from the chair and throw him out—all six feet, two inches of him.

In a second, she realized her mistake. He raised his head, a mischievous grin spreading across his lips. There wasn't time to stop the impetus of her forward rush. Nathan clamped his hand around her wrist and gave it a slight tug, sending her sprawling across his lap before she had a chance to struggle.

"Never get angry, sweet nymph, just get even," he instructed in a gentle whisper as his head dipped towards hers. Joanna only had time to turn her face away, but he wasn't deterred. His lips nestled in the hollow of her jawline while he released her hair from the barrette, allowing it to fall to her shoulders. "I thought you were going to hold up that fireplace all afternoon."

"I thought we were going to talk," she gasped out as Nathan's hand slipped through the wide neck opening of her shirt. He ran his finger tips in a light, teasing touch over the upper swell of her breasts. Her slightest movement would surely bring his playful fingers into contact with the hardening peak that betrayed her physical response to his feathery touch.

"Don't you realize by now that this is our best means of communication?" In spite of his husky words, he drew back. The tormenting hand moved to cup the side of her neck. Gently, but insistently his thumb urged her face up to meet his burning gaze. "I won't believe there's anyone, including Collins, who can reach you the same way I do. What we had in Nassau was unique, Joanna."

"What we had was a holiday fling based purely on plain, old, ordinary lust," she bit out in disgust. He couldn't know her derision was aimed more at her traitorous body than at his smooth, seductive words. Her mind knew he was lying again, but her body refused to listen.

"Lust, perhaps, sweetheart," he answered with a tempting smile, his eyes darkening to charcoal gray, "but there certainly wasn't anything plain or ordinary about it. Good Lord, I'm a reasonably healthy male, but surely you can't believe I could have made love to just any woman throughout the night. Our time together was the result of a very special chemistry."

"Oh." The weak thread of sound was all her confused mind could manage. The explanation didn't match her perception of Nathan's motives. Blinking owlishly up at him, she tried to come up with a suitable reply, then was stunned at the fatuous grin that spread over his face. Suddenly, she realized that he misinterpreted her silence. Surely he didn't think she was that naive?

He made a strange noise in his throat. "You didn't know; you really didn't know." His triumphant laughter rang out as he sprang to his feet, effortlessly holding her against his chest as he spun around. Joanna clutched at his broad shoulders when he suddenly dropped her to her feet. Before she could regain her balance, she was crushed against the wall of his chest.

"This is a seduction of a different color." With a soft laugh, he buried his face in her tousled hair. Then abruptly he set her free. Cupping her face between his hands, he gazed earnestly into her startled emerald eyes. "I want you, nymph, and I mean to have you, but we'll take it slowly. I see I've been rushing you. So, Joanna Trent, I'm giving you fair warning, you will be mine."

THREE

I'm going stark, staring mad, Joanna thought wildly when Nathan abruptly turned away, *or I'm still asleep and dreaming this farce.* Pinching herself didn't help because the tall, dark-haired man was still there. Since he seemed to be leaving, she started to relax slightly. Just as she was contemplating collapsing into the nearest chair, he turned back. She took a reflexive step backward as he walked toward her. One of them was crazy, and she was fairly sure it wasn't her.

He gave her an indulgent smile. "Don't worry, love, I won't pounce. I forgot to deliver Evan's message. You're going out with us this evening. I'll be back about seven o'clock."

"Who's us?" *Good heavens, there can't be more than one of him.* She knew she was being ridiculous.

"Evan, Helen, and me is us," Nathan explained, his expression slightly chagrined at his graceless invitation. "Now, don't ask too many questions. All I want to do right now is carry you to the nearest bed. We wouldn't be seen again for days. But, unfortunately for both of us, love, I'm going to be a very patient man."

Joanna didn't even wait for the sound of the slamming

47

door behind his retreating figure. She fell into the chair they'd shared only minutes earlier, wrapping her arms securely around her trembling body. Nathan barely touched her, but she felt as if he'd made love to her as thoroughly as he had in Nassau. Everything flew out of her mind whenever he was near her. She forgot his deceit and her righteous anger for a charming smile and a passionate kiss.

"A mature woman should know better," she told herself in disgust. That was exactly what happened to her roommate in college. Maureen let herself be fooled by charm, personality, and good sex, until the night before graduation when she told Garth Hamilton IV that she was pregnant. A factory worker's daughter was good enough as a play thing, but not for marrying into the prominent Hamilton family, especially when they owned the factory. After spending a tearful night with Joanna and Jennifer, Maureen had gone out the next morning to run her car into a train.

Maureen's funeral brought even further disillusionment for Joanna. Her grief over her friend brought an end to her own engagement. She discovered a side of Keith that she never knew existed. He took Garth's side, standing not three feet from Maureen's family. He was just another pampered son, who thought more of his family's position than he did for someone's feelings. As he tried to excuse his heartlessness, Keith dealt one last blow. His family was still trying to accept Joanna's being an adopted child, though the Trent's pedigree was helping to win them over. After Maureen's funeral, she'd never seen Keith again, though he pestered her for months.

The chimes from the bracket clock on the mantel snapped Joanna back to the present. Nathan would be back in three hours. There wasn't any way she could refuse the invitation, and she didn't know where they were going.

The man was definitely a loon, she decided as she started pushing the furniture back in place. Interior decorating would have to wait while she prepared herself for battle against a wily and crazy opponent.

She wouldn't let him catch her off guard again. Nathan just couldn't stand to lose, so he was continuing his charade. What else could explain his determined pursuit? As soon as he succeeded in winning her over once more, he'd be off looking for a new conquest. But she had a secret weapon. Nathan didn't know that she was a woman who responded with cold, calm logic, not with emotion. Tonight Nathan Hartford was going to meet the real Joanna Trent.

With a cool smile of satisfaction, she walked purposely to her bedroom to select just the right dress for the evening.

Her confidence would have faltered slightly at the sight of her recent visitor still standing outside her door. All signs of his recent high spirits had vanished. Nathan thoughtfully contemplated the closed door as he shoved his hand into his jeans pocket, immediately touching the piece of paper he'd carried for two months. The note Joanna left for him in Nassau was now a wrinkled scrap with faded ink. He kept it with him for two months as a talisman to remind him of Joanna—a warm, responsive Joanna—since the morning he'd awakened alone and found the note on the dresser.

He thought he'd understood her sudden departure. What had happened between them had been surprising, impulsive, and a little frightening. Her hasty departure had only delayed his plan to deepen their relationship. However, he hadn't anticipated her coolness when they met again.

As he walked down the hallway, he considered the new Joanna. The only emotion he could define was apprehension. He didn't understand why she would be afraid of him, unless she was afraid of her emotional reaction to him. That was something he could sympathize with; he was still shaken by his own emotions. He'd only known her a few days in Nassau and seen her twice since then, but he knew what he wanted.

The bewildered look on her face that gave away her inexperience formed in his mind. His lips curved into an idiotic grin. The more he thought about Joanna's defensive attitude, the happier he became. Nathan was whistling by the time he reached his car. Tonight he would begin the siege that would breach the walls of Joanna's resistance. He'd show her that there wasn't any reason to be afraid of her feelings or a relationship with him.

Joanna felt her stomach twisting into knots as the electronic digits on the night stand flashed six fifty-nine. For a minute she wondered if she was going to have evening as well as morning sickness. As she reached for the soda crackers that she kept by the bed, her stomach settled back to normal. It was only nerves over the evening ahead.

The door bell rang a second later. As she went to answer the door she was amazed at how calm she felt. Her nervousness had been stage fright. Suddenly she was cool and aloof, ready to face anything.

"Good evening, Nathan," she said serenely. Running her eyes over his elegant dove gray suit, she ignored the musky scent of his cologne. Nathan Hartford was an exceptionally good-looking man, but that had nothing to do with the slight jump in her pulse rate.

"You need a warning from the Surgeon General, sweetheart," Nathan answered, seeing his good intentions going up in flames. The black sheath emphasized Joanna's lush curves, adding a glimpse of one spectacular leg through the slit skirt; the blouson bodice provocatively draped over her shadowed cleavage. Involuntarily he reached for her, his hands settling on the thin straps at her shoulders.

"Are we picking up your aunt and uncle?" Joanna asked and stepped back neatly out of reach.

Nathan found himself clutching a silk paisley shawl, instead of her warm, soft body. Draping the shawl over her shoulders, he noticed almost dispassionately that his hands were shaking as he lifted her hair from beneath the material. Her hair was styled exactly as it had been in Nassau, a jeweled barrette substituting for the silk orchid that was on his dresser.

"Anxious to start the evening, are we?"

"Naturally," Joanna replied, giving him a cool smile. "It's not often one gets the opportunity of an evening on the town, no matter who is her escort." She hesitated for a minute when his hands tightened on her shoulders. "Shall we go? I wouldn't want to keep your charming relatives waiting."

"I think we'd better," Nathan muttered as he followed her out the door, "before we run out of small talk."

Joanna agreed wholeheartedly. She was winning at this point, but it wouldn't last. She needed the protection of other people before he had a chance to retaliate.

"I'm sure you and Helen will find plenty to talk about." Nathan's comment broke the uneasy silence that lasted most of the trip to the hotel. "Comparing my faults alone should keep the two of you busy for the greater part of the night."

"Doesn't she approve of you either?" Joanna asked without thinking. The question hung in the air as he went around the car to open her door.

"On the contrary, she thinks I'm perfect, except that I'm not married. That alone is enough to deserve her censure. She's a dyed-in-the-wool matchmaker."

"I suppose if you ever turn in your bachelor spurs, you

might attain sainthood again?" Joanna allowed herself one final shot with Evan and Helen Hartford only a few feet away.

"Careful, love," Nathan whispered in her ear, his breath warming her skin. "Remember, you still have to go home. At this rate, neither of us will end up unscathed."

"Joanna, my dear, I'm so glad you could come with us on such short notice," Evan boomed as he extended his hand. "Helen's been dying to meet you."

"I'm the pygmy on the left," announced a light soprano voice. "I've heard so many nice things from Evan and Nathan. I was bursting with curiosity, but I do wish you were a bit shorter."

Joanna warmed to the other woman immediately. Next to the two men and herself, Helen's five feet, one inch figure was indeed dwarfed. What Helen lacked in size, however, didn't deter her from tackling either her nephew or her husband. Joanna watched with interest as the older woman lectured Nathan for not calling his mother more often.

"You'll adore my partner, Diane. She keeps threatening to chop me off at the knees," she told Helen with an understanding smile.

"Ah, a woman after my own heart," Helen exclaimed, giving Joanna a triumphant smile in return. She patted her silver gray chignon absently after Evan helped her into her muslin jacket. Her blue eyes twinkled impishly, reflecting her royal blue dress. "Have these two deigned to tell you where we're going? No? Well, I'm not budging from this spot without knowing our destination."

Two pairs of masculine gray eyes met over her head before they answered in unison. "The Goldenrod Showboat, your ladyship."

Helen gave an indignant sniff and hooked her arm through Joanna's to lead her quickly away. "I hate it when they do that. At least Evan doesn't pat me on the head any more. The last time I bit him.'' Her very real satisfaction with the accomplishment set off Joanna's stifled laughter. ''Not so loud. I'm not forgiving them until we get in the car.''

When they were all seated comfortably Joanna wondered why Nathan started the engine but didn't leave the parking lot. Instead he turned, along with his uncle, to regard Helen as she gazed absently out the back window. With studied unconcern she turned to look at the two men in the front seat. ''I'm all done. Let's get this show on the road.''

''You'll get used to it, Joanna,'' Evan explained with an affectionate chuckle as he turned to face forward again. ''That was only a minor infraction, sometimes she sulks for an hour, if we really misbehave.''

Helen shrugged. ''I have to do something, or they overpower me. Evan has five brothers, and Hartfords only come in one size, large.''

''They get just what they deserve,'' Joanna asserted with a meaningful look at the back of Nathan's head. She was having a wonderful time watching Helen handle the two men. Anyone that got the better of a Hartford male was her friend for life.

Helen dismissed the two men with a wave of her hand. Within minutes she had Joanna talking about her work and family. Caught off guard, Joanna mentioned George without thinking, but realized it was a common name. She sighed in relief when Nathan captured his aunt's attention. A few more minutes and she would have undoubtedly been telling Helen about the baby.

''Did Evan tell you the big news?''

''I left that for you, Nat,'' Evan interrupted, clearing his throat and giving his wife an uneasy look over his shoulder.

"Well, what is it?" Helen prompted impatiently when Nathan hesitated.

"You can start paring down your list of eligible young ladies," he started, watching her in the rearview mirror. "I'm moving to St. Louis permanently."

"What?" Both women spoke at the same time. Joanna knew Helen's outrage was feigned, but hers was from outright terror. She'd been relying on Nathan only being in St. Louis on a temporary basis; hoping once the Hartford takeover was running smoothly, he would go back to Philadelphia where he belonged. But now he was staying.

Unconsciously her hand went to her abdomen. How much time did she have before she began to show? She needed to start reading up on pregnancy very soon. She also needed to get Nathan Hartford out of her life as soon as possible. Tonight she would have to go beyond her usual cool but companionable facade that her other escorts knew too well. She would have to become an iceberg. All Nathan's seductive overtures would be as ill fated as the maiden voyage of the *Titanic*.

Evan's voice brought Joanna out of her frantic thoughts. "We've decided Nathan will take over the complete operation here to prepare for when I retire."

"What are your mother and I going to do for entertainment? If we aren't around to dig up prospective brides, who knows what you'll come up with on your own." Helen's expression was serious, but her eyes were twinkling with suppressed amusement, implying that Nathan had the judgment of a twelve-year-old.

"I don't plan to pick up the first female that comes down the street." Nathan's indignant reply was barely heard over the others' laughter. "If you get too worried, call Joanna for a progress report."

"Really, Nathan, you certainly have more than your share of the Hartford arrogance," Helen complained.

"Joanna has better things to do than keep track of your love life."

"Then you'll just have to trust me."

"In a pig's eye. Your mother and I will take turns visiting," Helen declared with authority. "That way I can watch you, and it will give me an excuse to see Joanna again."

"Now that that's settled, we can enjoy ourselves," Evan offered, giving an exaggerated sigh of relief as Nathan parked on the levee. "Ladies, watch your step."

The dark, noisy interior of the theater was the ideal way to spend the evening, Joanna decided as she took her seat around the table that Nathan miraculously found in the balcony. She could sit back and enjoy herself without becoming involved in personal conversations. Soon she willingly joined in booing and hissing with the rest of the audience whenever the villain appeared and cheering for the stalwart hero. Some braver souls yelled insults and questions at the actors that were deftly fielded.

A warm hand grazing the bare skin of her back abruptly drew Joanna's attention from the stage. The spark that traveled along her nerve endings instantly recognized Nathan's touch. At the familiar bristled softness of his mustache against her cheek, Joanna snapped her head to the side.

"I hope white wine is innocuous enough, nymph?"

His low, seductive tone made her glance in alarm at the older Hartfords across the table, but they were still involved in the play. Joannna decided that the only way to survive the evening was to ignore Nathan's innuendos. He couldn't know she had to swear off alcohol as well as caffeine. The reference was to her near abstinence in Nassau. She should have known he wouldn't give up easily.

The rest of the performance was a blur, though she pretended to pay rapt attention. All she could remember later was the hot, electric contact of Nathan's hand moving insidiously up and down her bare spine above the edge of her dress. She didn't dare object and draw Helen and Evan's attention away from the play. Each time the molten knot at the base of her stomach became too much to bear, she moved out of reach. Nathan countered every move, testing her endurance by pressing his hard thigh against her silk covered leg. She almost let out a moan of relief when the curtain finally went down. Evan gave her a temporary reprieve by sending Nathan ahead to secure a table for the Dixie Land Band on the lower level.

Nathan's slanted smile mocked her efforts as Joanna carefully seated herself between Evan and Helen. She had the satisfaction of confusing him when she asked for a club soda.

"Now, Joanna, what do you recommend for sightseeing while I'm in town? Evan's going to be tied up in meetings, even tomorrow," Helen explained when the band took a break a short time later.

"Let's see there's the zoo, the Arch and the Jefferson Expansion park," Joanna began, then stopped to apologize when her foot bumped into someone else's under the small, round table.

"That's perfectly all right," Nathan put in smoothly, smiling at her over his drink.

Joanna didn't trust his guileless look, but went on with her list of attractions. "There's the renovation of Union Station and all the shops," she hesitated again when something touched her leg. This time she knew it wasn't an accident because a shoeless foot was rubbing against her leg. She kicked out in Nathan's direction and was immediately contrite when Evan grunted in pain.

After apologizing she went on, not daring to move again or look at Nathan. "If you want history and antiques, there's St. Charles."

"Stop right there," Helen exclaimed over Evan's groan of despair.

Joanna barely heard Evan's complaints about the dent in his checkbook. By now her total sense of touch was centered in her legs as Nathan gave them both thorough attention. He just discovered an erogenous zone at the side of her ankle that she never knew existed.

"I'd love to visit St. Charles. Joanna, are you free tomorrow?" Helen asked, ignoring her husband's protests. "Evan and Nathan have clients coming in tomorrow, and I'd just get in their way."

Joanna nodded. She was afraid to open her mouth. Nathan had worked his way up to the back of her knee. Closing her eyes against the exquisite feeling, she blocked out his innocent smile that didn't match the devilish look in his eyes.

"Joanna, is that you?" A familiar voice traveled over the babble of conversations around their table. Joanna snapped her eyes open.

"Chris, Brian!" She jumped to her feet and waved to the slim redhead who was leading a raven haired man through the tables. The sight of her friends had never been so welcome. "What are you doing here?"

"We're celebrating our wedding anniversary," the grinning woman announced as soon as they reached the table, "and another addition to the Judson family."

Good heavens, it's an epidemic, Joanna mused before she hugged the couple with great enthusiasm. They'd allowed her to escape Nathan's torment gracefully. "Wonderful. My godson is going to get a new brother or sister. When?"

"Around Thanksgiving, I just found out this morning," Chris supplied eagerly, eyeing the three Hartfords with interest.

I wonder if we'll go into labor at the same time. Joanna

squelched the thought as Chris cleared her throat. "Oh, I'm sorry. Chris and Brian Judson, this is Evan and Helen Hartford and Nathan Hartford."

"Nice to meet you." Chris gave Nathan a thorough inspection before giving her friend an assessing look. "Where do you find them, Jo?"

"Chris." Brian's scolding tone blended with Joanna's as he shook hands with Evan and Nathan.

"Evan and Nathan are new clients," Joanna put in hastily, hoping Chris wouldn't say anything else outrageous.

"Not another one," Chris chided with a saucy wink. "You said that the last time with that gorgeous South American. Have you given up dating altogether?"

"Very funny." Joanna was thinking rapidly for a way to head Chris off. Nathan's mustache was twitching with amusement, his eyes never leaving her face. "How's little Jeffrey? It must be at least three weeks since I saw him."

"Why not come back to the house and see for yourself?" Brian included everyone in the invitation, sinking Joanna's hopes of separating the two groups. The thought of Chris and Nathan together for any length of time was frightening. The least of her worries was the Judsons mentioning that George was her brother.

"Joanna, you and Nathan go ahead," Helen put in. "I've been dying to get a certain person to take me dancing, and this gives me the perfect chance. Our hotel has a lovely band."

Helen wouldn't back down when the others protested, especially her husband. Nathan and Joanna would drop the older couple at their hotel, then join the Judsons. Joanna maneuvered desperately for a moment alone with Chris. Luck was finally with her as they were jostled in the crowd at the entrance, leaving the Hartfords behind momentarily.

"Client, hmmm? Do you always get on a first name basis with their relatives?" Chris teased as they moved toward the outside door. "I've heard business is rewarding, but Nathan is a nice bonus. He looks like a definite maybe."

"Not now, please," Joanna begged. "This is not a man I want you to tease or quiz about his personal life. This is my biggest account, and tonight is strictly business. He doesn't need to be bored to death with your opinion of my social life. Please, Chris?"

"All right, if it's that important, but it's such a shame."

"Oh, and if George's name comes up, don't mention that he's my brother either," Joanna added as an afterthought.

"What scheme has he inveigled you into this time?"

"Nothing serious, Brian. It's really nothing important, but it would complicate things right now," she hissed as the Hartfords came into view.

After dropping Evan and Helen at the hotel, Joanna braced herself for whatever Nathan planned next. She was acutely aware of his every move, waiting for him to renew his assault.

Nathan clenched his hands on the steering wheel, battling his conscience over his behavior on the showboat. He promised himself he'd move slowly but had succumbed to his baser instincts. Now he needed to make amends.

"Known the Judsons long?" he asked, grasping at the first thing that came to mind.

"Brian, yes; Chris, no," Joanna replied absently.

"How interesting." Nathan cursed under his breath. He really needed to repair the damage he'd done if Joanna was only going to answer in monosyllables.

"Hmmmm? Oh," Joanna exclaimed when his dry tone broke into her thoughts. "Brian's like an extra brother. His sister Jennifer was my best friend in elementary school, so I've known him since I was kid."

"Does Jennifer live in the area?" Nathan continued,

latching onto the subject like a lifesaver. This should keep him out of trouble until they reached the Judsons'.

"No, she's married, finally as her brother would say, and lives near New Orleans. We still get together on holidays. She and Chris are pretty close. They worked together at the architectural firm where Brian did his apprentice work."

"Pretty nice set up," Nathan replied with a chuckle. *This is good, keep going, old man.* **She's** *relaxing and talking naturally just like she did in Nassau.* "Sounds like Jennifer had a chance to break in her sister-in-law ahead of time."

"Actually, if it hadn't been for Jennifer, they might not have gotten married."

"Another matchmaker surfaces. Helen started with my uncle David in 1939 and just kept going. She married off my sister last fall."

"Well, Jennifer only helped things along," Joanna stated in defense of her friend. "Heaven only knows how long they'd have stumbled on by themselves. We merely sped them along."

"You, too?" Nathan asked with interest as he switched lanes to avoid a car that shot out of a side street. "You women certainly start at an early age."

"For this one, yes. Otherwise, I try to leave well enough alone. Relationships get screwed up enough without anyone interfering. Most of my friends seem to hit the rocks too often all by themselves."

Nathan didn't like the sudden pessimistic turn to the conversation. "What was so intriguing about Chris and Brian?"

"The two of them were crazy about each other, but Chris was only telling Jen, while Brian was crying on my shoulder," Joanna said, the reminiscent smile on her face giving Nathan a pang of envy. "He would moon around, watching her every move when she wasn't looking. Naturally, Chris was doing the same thing. After a year of silent suffering, we had to do something or as Jennifer said, they both would have gotten fired. They were both more preoccupied with each other than their work."

"So, how did you manage?"

Joanne started to giggle, a sound that Nathan had been longing to hear for two months. "We locked them in the bedroom of a model home for two hours. Brian cracked after the first hour."

"And they lived happily ever after," Nathan finished, joining in her amusement. "Couldn't they really have managed by themselves?"

"I doubt it. They both had too much pride to stick their necks out beyond casual friendship, even though they were both hurting." Her voice was suddenly thoughtful, all traces of laughter gone. "There's probably hundreds of relationships that never started because no one wanted to stick their necks out emotionally."

"That sounds about right," Nathan answered, matching her tone. Her words were hitting close to home. He was still dancing around Joanna, testing the waters before he declared his feelings. "Most people aren't going to allow themselves to be vulnerable to the pain of possible rejection. I've got a friend who gets so worked up just asking a woman for a date, that he hardly ever asks anyone to go out. He turns into a basket case without even talking to the woman."

"That doesn't surprise me," Joanna commented, then broke off whatever she was going to say. "There's the turn at the next light."

The rest of the trip was made in thoughtful silence.

"Come on in. Brian's walking the babysitter home," Chris called from the doorway as they came up the front walk. Her next words horrified Joanna. "This is the first chance I've gotten to ask about your trip to Nassau. You can fill me in on all, and I mean all, the details while the guys talk sports or something.''

Joanna knew the moment Chris invited them to the house that it was a bad move. She was saved by Brian sprinting up the front walk. ''Could I interest anyone in a little libation? Nathan, what's your pleasure?''

Chris signaled to Joanna as the men walked over to the bar. She followed the other woman upstairs, wondering how soon she could make an excuse to leave. Besides the ever present danger of Chris asking the wrong question, Joanna was beginning to tire. However, right now was not the time to ask for any advice on the first months of pregnancy. First thing Monday morning she'd make an appointment with Dr. Jessop and get some confidential advice until she decided exactly how she was going to handle her condition.

Chris turned into the first room at the top of the stairs, tiptoeing cautiously, but groaned as soon as she crossed the threshold. Joanna understood why at the sight of Jeffrey standing upright, holding firmly onto the side of the crib. His blue eyes blinked at them from under a thatch of black hair, the image of his father. For the first time, she wondered who her baby would look like, his father or his mother.

''I swear this kid has built-in radar that wakes him up the second we walk into the house. I must be crazy for having another one. This guy's a handful all by himself.'' Chris gave an exaggerated grunt as she hauled her hefty son into her arms. ''Brian told me the day Jeff was born that he'd be a football player, and I'm becoming a believer.''

''Anjo,'' Jeff sputtered in reply, reaching out for Joanna. Both women were still laughing over his antics when they rejoined the men downstairs. Chris pulled a face at the sight of Nathan and Brian ensconced by the fireplace, arguing over the merits of their respective hockey teams. Jeff came to the ladies' rescue by screaming hello, startling the sports fans. Amid the laughter, Brian introduced his son.

"Hey, Chris, if he keeps this up we can back him for the hog calling contest at the state fair."

"Sorry about your eardrums, Nathan. I didn't have a chance to warn you." Chris ignored her husband as Jeff wiggled his arms towards Nathan as if he was a new toy. "He's never met a stranger."

"Don't worry, I'm used to this," Nathan reassured her, and he expertly transferred his new friend into his arms. "In the Hartford clan, there's a baby about this size and vocal range every year. Grandfather woke up one day with seventeen grandchildren, and now twelve of them have at least one baby a piece."

Joanna dropped into the nearest chair and watched in fascination as Jeff fumbled with Nathan's lapel, then investigated his pockets. She was surprised at the lump in her throat at the sight of the tall man holding the squirming boy.

"You're out of luck there, pal. Uncle Nat didn't come prepared this time. I'm fresh out of goodies."

Jeff was disenchanted, twisting around to look for new territory. "Anjo!"

Joanna went to the rescue reluctantly. There was a disturbing intimacy about taking the toddler from Nathan's arms. She was also slightly envious of Nathan's large family, and she refused to think about how he'd respond to a child of his own. "Your family reunions must be a mad house."

"Not once you get the names straight. My sister's been married less than a year, and her husband is about fifty percent right so far. Now he's working on the out-of-towners.''

Jeff was put to bed, reassured his parents were home, and the four adults settled down in the family room. While Nathan asked about Brian's architectural work, Joanna had trouble keeping her eyes open. She let Chris ramble on about her latest discount shopping find, resting her head against the back of the couch. The others talked quietly for another hour as she slept peacefully.

"Come on, sleepy head, it's time for the rest of us to get some sleep," Nathan said as he woke her gently. "Besides, Helen will never forgive me for wearing you out before she gets a chance at those antiques tomorrow."

"Oh, no," Joanna groaned, flushing in embarrassment at the others' indulgent laughter. "I didn't."

"Oh, yes, you did," Chris confirmed with a giggle. "Don't worry, though; you're among friends. I do this all the time when I'm pregnant. You've been pushing yourself again, haven't you?"

"Not really. It's just been a bad week with Fred out sick, and I decided to clean house today," Joanna mumbled, still not fully awake as Nathan draped her shawl around her.

"If you cleaned more often, it wouldn't tire you out so much." Chris's teasing voice was the last thing Joanna remembered until she felt someone nudging her. This time she was going to be stubborn. She deserved her rest. Since she was so comfortable, she burrowed deeper into her pillow until it spoke to her. "Joanna, we can't sit out here all night. What will the neighbors think?"

"Not again?" she moaned without moving.

"Yes, again," was Nathan's amused reply. "Come on, up you go. My shoulder's getting stiff."

"How long have we been here?" she asked as he propped her against the passenger door. She began to drift off again as Nathan walked around the car. The opening door brought her back to her senses.

"Long enough for the lady on the first floor to peek out of her curtains twice." Nathan chuckled as he lifted her bodily out of the car. He leaned her against the car while he closed the door.

"Ah, Mrs. Lefkowitz." Joanna giggled as she thought about the octogenerian who lived below her. "This is probably the high point of her week. She thrives on romance, real or imagined, a real soap opera addict."

"Let's really give her some romance then." Nathan swept a wavering Joanna off her feet.

"You're insane, certifiably insane," she murmured with a sleepy chuckle, letting her head rest comfortably on his shoulder, despite his questionable mentality. She relived the strange protected feelings she'd experienced the first time he carried her in his arms in Nassau.

"Yes, but Mrs. Lefkowitz will adore it."

"Mmmmm." She knew when they reached the top of the stairs and impulsively asked the question that had been teasing her half the evening. "How did you get your shoe back on so fast?"

"Get out your key, Joanna."

Once the door was unlocked, she returned to her question. She stretched back as far as her arms would allow, her fingers twined tightly together around his neck. Her arch look was more owlish than intimidating. "Well?"

"I dropped my cocktail napkin while you were hugging the expectant parents."

"How ingenious," she decided, sighing in admiration and answering his endearing grin with a soft smile. Recklessly she kicked her shoes off with a flip of each foot. She was thinking of palm trees and steel-rim band music. Absently she began loosening his tie. "Do you take super vitamins? You must, since you persist in carrying me."

"It's all done with mirrors. Which way is the bedroom? You'll never make it on your own." Nathan's voice was husky and slightly uneven.

"Second on the left, the light's on." Her head drifted back to the solid comfort of his shoulder. Once she managed to unfasten his tie, her hand began wandering over his chest.

"Joanna." He sounded strange as she blinked up at him. She watched his mouth in fascination as she tried to understand his words. "Where's your nightgown?"

"Don't wear one, but don't tell anyone. They'd never believe you." She snuggled her face back into his neck when that was settled. His arms tightened momentarily as a groan of despair rose in his throat. "Nathan, are you all right?"

"Joanna, can you stand by yourself?"

"Do I have to?" She opened her eyes halfway in bewilderment and looked around. "Oh, we're here already. I'm thirsty."

"Yes, sweetheart, now let go of my neck. That's it. Now, turn around, and I'll unzip you." She obeyed his instructions without hesitation. When the task was accomplished, he lifted her hand and placed it against the front of her dress to hold it in place. Then he turned her to face him again.

Joanna stared down at her hand with interest. When he called her name, she looked up at him obediently. He was saying something about a glass of water and the bed. She nodded as if she understood before he turned away. When he disappeared into the bathroom, she tried to think about what she was supposed to do, but the intriguing presence of Nathan in her bedroom distracted her.

He wanted her to take off her dress. She smiled in triumph, and let her arm fall to her side, allowing the loosened straps to slide off her shoulders. The black material slithered to the floor. She was still staring happily down at the rumpled dress when Nathan returned.

He froze in the doorway of the bathroom when he saw Joanna standing next to her brass bed, covered only by her black lace bikini briefs and black panty hose. His muffled oath called her attention to his still form.

"You came back," she exclaimed in welcome. "Are you going to tuck me in?"

_____ FOUR _____

Nathan was acting very strangely, Joanna decided as he seemed to leap across the room. He snapped back the bedspread and sheet, snarling at her to "Get in." She barely had time to scramble into bed before the sheet was thrown over her, blanketing her entire body and her head. Pulling back the cotton sheet, she peered over the edge of the sheet to find him holding out a glass of water. To please him, she obediently drank half the water. If she behaved, maybe it would erase the fierce scowl on his face. When she handed him the glass, he put it on the night stand and turned to leave.

"No good-night kiss?" Joanna asked petulantly before he could take a step. Her hazy dream wasn't going right. He wasn't supposed to leave. The elegant cherry canopied bed in her dreams always held two people.

Against his better judgment, Nathan turned back to the bed. He knew that he should be walking out the door right now. Joanna was staring at him with the innocent eyes of a child, but he couldn't forget the womanly body that was hidden beneath the thin sheet. "Do you know what you're asking?"

"Well, of course, stupid. You can't tuck someone into bed without a kiss. It just isn't done."

Groaning under his breath, he sat on the side of the bed, carefully keeping as much space between them as possible. Unfortunately, that didn't satisfy Joanna. She reached up and linked her arms around his neck. Bracing his arms on either side of her shoulders, he tried to maintain his rigid control. He couldn't take advantage of Joanna in this childish state, no matter how provocative she was. He would stick to his earlier resolve to take things slowly.

But it wasn't a child who kissed him. When he brushed his mouth against hers, her lips parted in invitation. She increased the pressure when he kept his mouth firmly closed. Determinedly she nibbled on his lower lip, then soothed the wound with the slow movement of her tongue. He tried to pull back, but she held him in place with the dangling ends of his tie. She continued to probe his lips coaxingly. Nathan shuddered in reaction to her slender hand slipping through the opening of his shirt, grazing his feverish skin with her fingertips.

When her hand wandered further, skating over his rib cage, Nathan gave up the fight. His tormentor sighed in satisfaction as he pressed back against her tormenting tongue. Awkwardly he dealt with the sheet that separated their bodies, cupping the inviting swells of her ample breasts in his hands. Not content, he reluctantly released her mouth to trail his lips slowly downward for more intimate contact.

Joanna gasped with pleasure as his moist mouth replaced his teasing fingers at the aroused tips of her breasts. Urgently she pushed his jacket and shirt off his shoulders, and he abandoned his questing massage of her abdomen and hips to help. Moments later she felt the demanding weight of his taut body pushing her into the mattress.

Feverishly she kneaded the straining muscles of his lower back to delve beneath his waistband, arching herself into his hardening desire to express her need.

Simultaneously he reached for her lace briefs and panty hose while she fumbled with his belt buckle. Still pressed hip to hip, they raced to undress each other.

Joanna's impassioned whispers increased at the feel of Nathan's naked skin against her own. She'd dreamed of this for so long, thinking he was lost to her forever. Urging him to hurry, she grasped his hips, pulling him to her. She cried out his name as he entered her, the sound muffled as their tongues intertwined in a pantomime of their lower bodies. For a moment they lay perfectly still, the furious need that hurried their foreplay was momentarily sated.

Joanna caressed the smooth contour of Nathan's back, savoring the sensation of their joined bodies as he softly kissed every inch of her soft skin within reach. Slowly he began to move, languid movements that had her twisting restlessly beneath him. She pleaded with him to increase the pace, reaching for his hips, but he refused.

Joanna wanted, *needed* more. She let her hands speak for her, caressing his straining arms, his chest, his stomach. The tempo of his driving hips increased, but she didn't stop. He was giving her such joy that she wanted to reciprocate. Tangling her fingers in his thick hair, she pulled his wandering mouth to hers. They were almost at the peak, and she took them over the edge with a soulful kiss.

Their shared cries of completion were captured by their joined lips. Neither moved or spoke, unwilling to break the magic, exhausted from their mutual pleasure.

Nathan came to his senses first, sliding onto his side he gathered Joanna's soft body into his arms. He let the silence between them continue, unsure of himself in the aftermath of such an incredible moment. In spite of the elation he felt at reclaiming his passionate nymph, he experienced a twinge of guilt. Though she'd been the aggressor, he wasn't sure what Joanna really wanted.

He'd been patient for too long, forgetting that she didn't have two months of anticipating their meeting again. What was she feeling and thinking? Why did she leave Nassau so suddenly? What had gone wrong in the two months of their separation?

Bending his head to ask all his pent up questions, he let out a groan of renewed frustration. His temptress was asleep. With a regretful sigh, he pulled the sheet over their damp bodies. After waiting this long, he reasoned as he drifted off to sleep, he could be patient until morning.

Joanna smiled in pleasure as she snuggled against the hard body of her dream lover. Last night he'd been more spectacular, more demanding than ever before. She didn't want to wake up and find herself alone in bed. Keeping her eyes tightly closed, she reached for him, hoping to prolong—

Her eyes snapped open at the feel of warm skin beneath her palm. In horror, she stared into the chest of a very real, very male body. She jerked back and wished she hadn't when her stomach protested at the sudden movement. This wasn't the dream that haunted her since Nassau, this was a nightmare. She was in bed with Nathan Hartford, and she couldn't move without feeling nauseated.

Grappling with what to do next, she stared at the slumbering man in fascination. Luckily, he slept like a log. The sheet was draped carelessly over his hip as he lay on his side, almost in the same pose as when she'd first seen him. She'd opened her eyes to find him beside her on the float in the middle of the hotel's secluded cove. He'd teased her with his wicked smile and almost nonexistent swim trunks.

However, he wasn't a charming stranger anymore. He was the one man who could awaken her body to a level of excitement that she never knew existed. He was the man who'd deceived her about his identity. He was also the father of her child, who was making its presence known in the most unpleasant way.

Damn his conceited hide, Nathan had his revenge after all. Last night he proved that he could have her whenever he wanted. He'd won, just as he predicted. She didn't want to see his arrogant, triumphant smile that proved what a fool she'd been once again. Well, he wasn't going to have Joanna Trent for a play thing. She wasn't going to make the same mistake a third time.

Allowing her resurgent pride to take over, she gave him an angry shove, her anger giving her strength to move his dead weight. With a smug smile she watched in satisfaction as he rolled over the side of the bed. Just as he disappeared over the edge his gray eyes flashed open in surprise, then he landed on the floor with a satisfying thud. Some very enlightening invectives rose from the carpet. Curious, she carefully scooted to the side of the bed and peered over, but jumped back, clutching the sheet to her naked breasts as Nathan sat up.

"You did that on purpose. Are you crazy?" he yelled, looking angry and confused as he rubbed his shoulder, glaring at her unrepentant face.

"Not anymore, you over-sexed pig," she shouted back, ignoring the rolling of her stomach and pulling the sheet up to her neck defensively. "Get the hell out of my apartment before I decide to inflict further damage."

"Joanna—" he started in a coaxing tone as he levered himself to his feet.

"Don't try any of your slimy tricks on me, mister. Just

get out of my sight." She stared fixedly at his left shoulder
to block out the rest of his disturbing nude body. Guilt
was beginning to undermine her anger. She really shouldn't
have pushed him, but she couldn't let him stay here while
she crammed soda crackers in her mouth or ran for the
bathroom.

He gave her a searching look. She held her breath,
afraid he'd ignore her demands, afraid she might be sick
before he left. She almost sagged in relief when he bent
to pick up his scattered clothing. Without moving a muscle, she waited in rigid apprehension as he hastily dressed.
It took forever for him to pull on his pants and shirt. He
turned back to her tense figure after picking up his coat
and tie. Joanna simply pointed an unsteady finger toward
the door.

"Lady, you owe me one hell of an explanation," he
snapped, his anger quickly rising to match hers. "One
way or the other, we're going to have this out. You can
depend on it."

His threat hung in the air as he spun on his heel and
stomped out of the room. Joanna stared at the empty doorway, not moving until she heard the slam of the front
door. The noise released all the tension in her body, and
she grabbed for the package of soda crackers on the night
stand. She fumbled with the wrapping, reducing the square
crackers to crumbs in a matter of seconds.

Laying back against the pillows, she stared up at the
ceiling, munching vigorously on the crackers for temporary relief. A sudden flash of Nathan's stunned expression
as he rolled over the side of the bed started a giggle in
the back of her throat. Even as laughter shook her body,
she knew that it was the beginning of hysteria, not humor.
What had she done to herself now?

Two months ago her life had been neat, well-organized.
Then she'd gone to Nassau to recover from a virulent case

of flu. Had the virus caused brain damage? Was that why she'd suddenly felt the need to do something reckless? She'd been off balance from the moment Nathan Hartford appeared on the float. If she'd been in her right mind she'd never have done something so dangerous. A vacation affair was the last thing anyone, especially Joanna, would expect from her.

Sitting up slowly, testing the steadiness of her stomach, Joanna wiped her face with the back of her hand. She couldn't sit around crying over split milk. She had spent a week with Nathan, six days and seven glorious nights before she'd been frightened by her own emotions. Always so independent, she'd found herself waiting expectantly to see him every moment they were apart. She'd cut her vacation short, ruthlessly severing all ties with the man who was becoming an addiction.

Now he was back in her life and she knew that he'd tricked her. Why? Why hadn't he told her who he was? She hugged her knees to her chest and stared thoughtfully into space. Unfortunately, the longer she thought, the more she remembered about the night before. Burying her face in her knees, she could feel the hot rush of blood to her face. She knew exactly who was responsible for Nathan joining her in bed.

It was time that she gained some control of her life. After last night, Nathan wouldn't be chasing her anymore. He'd gotten what he'd wanted, proving that he was irresistible. She knew she should be relieved that he would be out of her life, but wondered why she felt sad instead of elated. Nathan would find another woman to enchant while she took care of her baby.

Joanna sat up and climbed out of bed. She would concentrate on the baby from now on. That was something concrete, something finite. Until now she'd been pretending that everything was normal. It wasn't something that was going to go away by ignoring it. Monday morning she'd call Dr. Jessup, then she'd tell Diane. She had to tell someone, get someone else's advice. She had to share the news with someone, and the father wasn't a likely candidate, at least not yet.

Nathan would have to be told sometime, but she couldn't do it right now. First she had to get used to planning for the baby.

"You know, Nathan, I didn't expect sparkling conversation this morning, but you've barely mumbled five words since you sat down," Helen Hartford remarked as the waiter refilled her coffee cup.

"Sorry, I didn't sleep very well last night. It must be the strange bed. I mean, I don't sleep very well in hotels," he finished weakly, grabbing his coffee cup like a life line. Drinking would keep him from making any other blunders.

"I know what you mean, dear. Hotel living is very unsettling," his aunt commiserated, unaware of his hidden meaning. "You'll be house hunting soon— Oh, there's Joanna, but who's that young man with her? Apparently she knows him fairly well."

Nathan followed the direction of Helen's gaze to the dining room entrance. The sight of Joanna kissing George Collins on the cheek didn't improve his mood, or the fact she seemed pleased to see the man. He felt some small satisfaction a moment later when Joanna's step hesitated slightly as she walked toward the table. It was the only sign she gave that she'd seen him sitting with Helen. Thankfully, Collins was waylaid by another engineer.

"Hello, dear, it's nice to have some pleasant company for a change. Nathan's been like a bear all through breakfast," Helen stated artlessly, gesturing for Joanna to take a seat. "What did you do to the poor boy last night?"

"Must be something he ate," Joanna said as she sat down in the chair farthest from the subject of their discussion. "I managed to disgrace myself by falling asleep at the Judsons' and on the way home in the car."

"Oh, Joanna, I wish I'd been there. After the years I've spent watching women throw themselves at the handsome devil, I'd love to have seen the one who couldn't be bothered to stay awake."

"In case anyone hasn't noticed, I'm still here," Nathan commented dryly, watching Joanna's averted face. She hadn't looked in his direction since she sat down.

"Sorry, dear, I know I sound like an unnatural aunt," Helen told without a tinge of remorse. "But I've seen two generations of Hartford men handling susceptible females too easily. It's very refreshing to have someone remind you that you're human occasionally."

"Now, Joanna, who was the nice looking young man I just saw you with?"

"Young man? Oh, George." She broke off as the waiter asked if she wanted to order breakfast.

"That's George Collins, Helen," Nathan continued while Joanna was preoccupied. "He's an engineer we inherited from Tri-Tex. He's been in Washington this week on a new project and flew in last night for today's meeting. He's also an old friend of Joanna's." The last words were grit out, finally getting Joanna to look at him. She seemed startled by his harsh tone, and it confused him even more.

What was going on in her convoluted, feminine mind? Why had she been so upset this morning after such a fantastic night? He didn't have any answers to the questions that had been careening around in his head all morning. The Joanna Trent he knew in Nassau had been replaced by someone he didn't understand, and he wanted to, desperately. He was becoming obsessed with solving the enigma of his Joanna.

That's exactly what she was, his. He knew that two months ago, and he knew it today. For some reason, she seemed to be afraid of him. Or was he right the other day, she was afraid of her own emotions? That tepid kiss she'd given Collins a few minutes ago was a travesty of emotion. It didn't compare to the passion she showed in his arms from the first time he'd kissed her. Somehow he had to get passed her apprehensions and show her she'd never be satisfied with a lukewarm relationship.

Though never known for his patience, he'd have to take things slowly, one step at a time. Whenever he thought he was gaining ground, he seemed to step back two paces, and every time it was due to his impatience. He'd thought they could pick up where they left off in Nassau, but Joanna had other ideas. This wasn't a normal relationship, and he didn't have any idea what to do next.

A normal relationship? That was the answer, he decided with a flash of inspiration. He would have to start all over again with Joanna, forget any intimacy between them. Nassau had been out of the ordinary, now they were back to reality. That was it. Joanna didn't trust what had happened in the Bahamas. He would have to work this as if they'd just met, and work slowly back towards the intimacy they'd already known.

"Earth to Nathan," his aunt's cheerful voice interrupted his thoughts.

"Sorry, Helen, I was just working out a problem," he answered, smiling for the first time that day. He looked directly at Joanna as he spoke, but she wouldn't meet his eyes.

"That's all right, dear. You can go back to it in a second. I just wanted to tell you we were leaving."

"Well, don't put too big a dent in Evan's checkbook.

Remember, everything you buy could mean overtime hours for Evan or me to pay off your debts," he remarked good-naturedly, his natural confidence returning quickly now that he'd solved his dilemma.

Helen didn't bother to answer, but gave a sniff and stood up, signaling to Joanna that she was ready to leave. She turned away, then glanced over her shoulder to give him a level stare. "That remark is going to cost you, nephew dear."

"That's just fine," he returned with a grin as they walked away. His mind wasn't on his aunt's threats, but the snug fit of Joanna's linen slacks as she walked out of the restaurant.

"That boy works too hard," Helen remarked as the two women crossed the lobby. "He needs a wife to get his mind off work occasionally."

"I understand that you're a thwarted matchmaker," Joanna returned absently, her mind on Nathan, but for a different reason. What had suddenly caused him to smile like that?

"Nathan, no doubt," Helen guessed without hesitation. "He's extremely smug about it because his parents met in London during the war. Since I wasn't involved with his parents' romance, he thinks he's immune."

"It's not immunity, in my opinion," Joanna responded, not guarding her tongue as she unlocked the passenger door of her car. "It's common, male conceit, which he's been handed in excess."

"Oh, Joanna, you're a woman after my own heart," Helen commented as the younger woman started the car. "You wouldn't be interested in taking on an attractive, but arrogant, young man?"

"No, thank you. It would be too much work." She tightened her grip on the steering wheel to keep her hands from shaking. This was going to be a long day. There had to be something besides Nathan that they could talk about. "Tell me about the Hartfords. There are six brothers, aren't there?"

"Yes, there's Thaddeus, Jason, Philip, David, Edgar, and of course my Evan. All are equally overpowering in their own way and their wives, myself included, are very independent ladies out of self-defense." Helen giggled like a school girl, reminding Joanna of the older woman's mock pout the night before. "The men try to be petty tyrants every once in while, but we won't stand for it. You're right, it is a lot of work, but it's worth it."

Joanna felt a stab of envy at Helen's contented sigh. It was apparent that Helen and Evan Hartford were still very much in love after thirty years of marriage. The prospect of her own single parenthood made her wistful for a moment, then she snapped out of it. She wasn't going to think about the baby or Nathan today. It was too dangerous. Helen was too sharp, and she needed to have her wits about her at all times. If she let down her guard for even a minute, she'd be telling the whole story to the sympathetic woman next to her.

With that in mind, Joanna launched into a discussion of Victorian furniture that would keep the conversation on safe, unthreatening ground.

Five hours later, Joanna was exhausted as she climbed the stairs to her apartment. The day had been enjoyable, but taxing. She'd had to guard every word, feeling guilty because she couldn't tell Helen that she was going to be a great-aunt by the end of the year. The ringing of the phone inside the apartment quickly distracted her from reliving the afternoon. Fumbling with the keys, she unlocked the door and ran to the phone.

"Joanna, where have you been? I've been calling you

for hours." Chris Judson barely waited for Joanna's breathless greeting.

"Helen Hartford and I went to St. Charles for the day, and I just got home. What's up?"

"What's up? You turn up with a devastating man, that you claim is a client, then swear Brian and I to secrecy without an explanation and you're off the next day taking the supposed client's aunt out all afternoon. You can't figure out why I called?"

"Chris, how did you ever learn to talk that fast?"

"Aw, Jo, have a heart. It's not nice to drive a pregnant woman crazy. What is going on?"

"Can you contain yourself until tomorrow night and come over for dinner?" Joanna asked, deciding that another expectant mother would be an excellent ally. There was a long, drawn out sigh at the other end of the phone. "Diane will be here, too, and I'll explain everything over a spaghetti dinner. How's that?"

"Terrible," Chris moaned. "I'm not sure I'll survive the next twenty-four hours, but if Diane's in on this, I suppose it can't be too awful."

Joanna knew Chris was going to be in for a shock. "Fine, how about six-thirty?"

"Okay. I'll leave Jeff and his daddy on their own for a change. This better be good," she warned before hanging up.

"You have no idea," Joanna answered dryly to the receiver.

"Order! Order!" Chris tapped her spoon against her water glass to get the others' attention at the end of dinner the next evening. "I'm demanding satisfaction. I've been the model guest. I helped set the table, brought the libation, and contributed my devastating wit to the dinner conversation. So, give."

"Well, I don't know. The libation, as you call it, was white grape juice." Joanna attempted to give serious consideration to the matter, though she was relieved she didn't have to explain why she'd sworn off alcohol. "What do you think, Diane?"

"It was interesting, but I think it was a little before its time." Diane studied the label carefully. "I don't think Wednesday, noon, is a good year, is it?"

"That is the finest sparkling Catawba grape from Herman, Missouri, I'll have you know. We tried some at Maifest last year, so we went back this weekend for a case. You have to make sacrifices when you're pregnant." Chris snatched the bottle away from her and stood up. She tried to look disdainful, but was having difficulty not joining in the others' laughter. "All right, you two comedians, I'm retiring to the drawing room, so bring your glasses."

"She's been into her Regencies again," Joanna whispered loudly as they followed Chris into the living room. She was ignored. When they were all seated, Chris merely stared balefully at her hostess. Taking a deep breath, Joanna didn't know if she was quite ready to make her confession yet. Or would she make it at all? What seemed so sensible yesterday was now terrifying.

She decided to start out slowly, working her way up to the big news of her pregnancy. "I give up. I met Nathan on vacation two months ago, and I'm not sure I want to continue anything but a business relationship, now that he's a client."

"That must please Nathan no end."

"Don't let her get too far ahead yet, Chris," Diane interrupted impatiently. "This is all I've heard so far, and I'm sure she's leaving out a few details. We're talking about a man, who's almost too good-looking to appear in GQ, and she acts like he's as exciting as day old bread."

"I know, the man makes my teeth sweat," Chris

agreed, giving the others a smug smile. "If I was single, I'd try to find a way to keep him around, not have some hang up about him being a client."

"Is Brian aware of this fixation of yours for strange men?" Joanna asked. She didn't know whether to laugh or cry over losing control of the conversation.

"Well, I'm thinking about telling him to grow a mustache," Chris shot back. "Quit stalling, what happened Saturday night after you left our house?"

"Jo, you didn't tell me you were with Nathan over the weekend," Diane accused, giving her friend a wounded look.

"Nathan is just trying to salvage his wounded male ego. I haven't been very receptive since we met again, and he's just trying to prove that he's irresistible. I'm battling outraged masculine dignity, pure and simple. Once I succumb to his charm again, he'll be off after a new patsy." She knew she was procrastinating. Maybe she could put off announcing her pregnancy until after her appointment with Dr. Jessup on Wednesday. After all, those pregnancy tests weren't always right, and her nausea in the morning could be something else.

"Honey, whatever is going on between you two has nothing to do with anyone's dignity," Diane charged as she refilled everyone's glass. "There's a few things you've left out, I'm sure, judging from the burning looks Nathan was giving you the night of the reception. I mean, I'd pledge my first-born male-child, if the man even—"

"Joanna, are you all right?" Chris broke in as Joanna began to cough uncontrollably.

"I'm fine," she answered breathlessly a minute later. "I just swallowed wrong, that's all." Joanna smiled weakly at the excuse, trying to reassure her friends. Her next words stuck in her throat when she looked at Diane. Her partner was staring at her in horrified fascination, her blue eyes as round as saucers. Chris looked just as dumbfounded, her mouth at half mast.

With studied calm, Joanna placed her glass on the coffee table as the silence in the room lengthened. Her two friends seemed to be frozen in place. "I suppose this is what is known as a pregnant pause?"

The bad joke did the trick. Both women came out of their stupor, speaking as one. "Joanna, you're pregnant."

"Have I come off my pristine pedestal?" she asked defensively. Her apprehensions over the matter were forgotten in her irritation. Why did everyone think she was a candidate for a nunnery, perhaps sainthood? She was as human as the next person.

"Don't be ridiculous. But how did—" Diane stopped herself, grimacing at the stupidity of what she was about to say.

"Oh, the usual way," Joanna returned, wondering why she was being flippant. These were her closest friends, and she'd anticipated their shock at the news. Then again, why was she aggravated with them, she wasn't exactly over the shock herself.

"What are you going to do? How does Nathan feel about it? When are you due?" Chris shot out the questions without waiting for the answers.

"Of course, Nathan doesn't know, and I haven't decided if I'm going to tell him."

"What?" the other two chorused, looking more stunned than they had at the first news.

"I only found out I was pregnant a little over a week ago. I'm not used to the idea myself," she started, enunciating each word carefully. "I'm having the baby and keeping it. Nathan and I had an affair in Nassau, nothing more. I never thought I'd see him again until he walked into the reception a week ago."

"You have to tell him, Jo. He's the father, for heavens'

sake," Diane exclaimed, becoming more agitated by the minute. "Even if you don't want to get married, he deserves to know he has a child."

"Get married? That's the farthest thing from his mind. I'm not going to marry some stranger because of some biological accident," Joanna announced, jumping to her feet and starting to pace around the room.

"He's not exactly a stranger," Chris put in dryly after Joanna had circled the room once.

"No, he's not. However, it's going to take more than a little diplomacy to handle this," Joanna stated, unconsciously crossing her hands over her stomach. She looked at Chris, then Diane, and turned back to Chris. Both women looked like members of a hanging jury. "Look, I did something stupid in Nassau. I decided to throw all caution to the wind and have an affair with a man I barely knew. Now I'm paying the consequences; however, that doesn't mean I have to become involved in a dead end relationship.

"I can afford to raise a child by myself. At first I was appalled that I was pregnant, but I'm gradually getting used to it. This is my baby, no one else's," she explained, but knew she wasn't doing a very good job from the skeptical looks on her friends' faces. "I didn't say I wouldn't tell Nathan, but just I wasn't sure I would."

"Okay, I think," Diane returned hesitantly, "but don't think we're going to drop the subject. We'll be terrific aunts to the little darling and royal pains to the mother."

"Are you sure Nathan just wants to have an affair? If Brian had given me some of those smoldering looks that Nathan gives you, I'd be celebrating more than my fifth anniversary."

"Nonsense, that's only frustration because I'm not falling under his spell again." Joanna ignored the little quiver down her spine at Chris's words. She'd been more susceptible to cool temperatures lately. It was just a draft in the room, that was all. "Ask Diane, she was around the first night he showed up."

"That's true," Diane concurred with apparent reluctance. "The sparks hit off both of them as soon as they were within twenty feet of each other but—"

"But what?" the other women prompted in unison; Chris in avid curiosity, and Joanna in surprise.

"There's something in what Chris says," Diane admitted sheepishly. "In fact, after that first night I said I didn't think it was only a bruised ego. You had him interested in Nassau. Besides, a week of orchids isn't the sign of an angry man."

"Orchids?" Chris's eyes lit up. "Now this is really promising stuff."

"If I didn't know Joanna better, I'd say she's afraid of this one," Diane confided, studying her friend closely. "I've watched her keep men at arms' length for years and stay very calm. Nathan had her trembling from across the room."

"I think you've hit it," Chris exclaimed, clapping her hands in excitement. "We've finally found the one that has Joanna breaking out in a cold sweat."

"Why don't you two go into business psychoanalyzing the love-lorn? Dear Abby would be shivering in her shoes at the competition," Joanna growled. If these were friends, she didn't need enemies. They'd gladly throw her at the first personable man with a gorgeous mustache and physique, just to laugh at her. "See if I help you with my dear brother now, Diane."

"You wretch," the blonde muttered as she flushed in embarrassment.

Chris cut ruthlessly through Diane's wail. "Are you finally going after George? I've been waiting for this since

Brian's birthday party, but we'll get to that in a minute.
I have just one more thing to say about Nathan.''

"All right." Joanna gave in under Chris's determined
stare, flopping down on the couch in defeat. She crossed
her arms over her breasts as she waited for her friend to
begin berating her again. "That's it, though, then it's on
to Diane and George."

"I think you should at least try to get to know Nathan
before you make a decision you'll regret. You've only
really known him a week. Nassau doesn't count," she
stated, but gave Joanna a chagrined smile. "Okay, it
counts. We are discussing his impending fatherhood.
However, you haven't really spent any time with him and
are basing your judgment on speculation. Will you agree
to that?"

Joanna didn't answer at first. She didn't know how to
answer. Her immediate reaction was an emphatic no, but
unfortunately, Chris was making sense. Her two friends
were watching her closely, and their concern was evident
by their worried expressions. "Yes, I'll agree to spend
more time getting to know Nathan."

"Good. Now, I'll admit that I lied. I have one last
question." Chris waited for Joanna's reluctant nod, grinning in anticipation. "Did Nathan leave your apartment
on Saturday night or Sunday morning?"

Joanna rolled her eyes in exasperation. She needed to
start picking friends who weren't so persistent. Then her
smile matched Chris's teasing grin as a suitable answer
came to mind. "Well, it was either very late Saturday
night or very early Sunday morning. It's all relative to
how you measure time. Satisfied?"

"Very funny," Chris shot back, sticking out her
tongue, but she relented and turned her attention to Diane.
"Now, tell me what you plan to do about George."

FIVE

"Oh, dear, I know Dr. Jessop confirmed that the bunny bit the dust yesterday, but do you have to wear mourning?" Diane announced from the doorway between her office and Joanna's. Her blue eyes moved disapprovingly over the stark black suit that covered Joanna from neck to mid-calf. The only relief was the back and white scarf that was draped over her right shoulder.

"They don't use rabbits anymore; it's all chemicals, I think. This is the power suit you helped me pick out for the Chamber of Commerce dinner last year, remember?" Joanna asked, turning back to the work table. She half-heartedly arranged the laminated ad samples on the polished surface of the conference table in front of her. Anything to stay busy. Nathan would be here soon, and she was a nervous wreck. "This suit is suppose to give me a feeling of authority, make me feel in control of every situation. So, why do I feel like Custer at the Little Big Horn?"

"Did we get up on the wrong side of the bed this morning?"

"In the royal vernacular, *we* almost didn't get up, because the alarm didn't go off, Princess Di. Once we felt human enough to get out of bed—after consuming an entire sleeve of crackers—our hair dryer shorted out with our hair partially dry," Joanna griped, waving her hand at her French plait. Leaning her hips back against the table, she crossed her arms over her breasts. "We also forgot to go grocery shopping after the phone call from the doctor yesterday, so we had bone dry bran flakes for breakfast. Then, our trusty carriage was almost out of gas, and everyone in town was ahead of us at the service station. We didn't get to work a half hour early as planned, but forty-five minutes late."

"I see. I'm tired from just hearing that recital," Diane managed after an exaggerated swallow, then began backing toward the door. "Why don't I just crawl back out the way I came in?"

"I'm sorry, Diane," Joanna said, letting her arms fall to her side, allowing her shoulders to sag dejectedly. "I shouldn't take it out on you. These things happen, but why did it have to happen today?"

"You're letting your imagination run away with you. Nathan isn't an ogre, and we have a dynamite presentation for Hartford Consolidated," she returned decisively before walking over to the walnut credenza behind Joanna's desk. "I think you need your caffeine ration about now," she stated, pointing to the fresh pot of coffee in the coffee maker. When Joanna nodded, she poured two cups and carried them to the teal blue tweed couch. "Now let's sit down and relax. Nathan won't be here for another fifteen minutes."

Joanna complied, joining her friend on the couch. Any diversion was welcome. After a half cup of coffee she felt less frazzled. "Thank heaven, this doesn't make me sick. Chris couldn't get near coffee during her last pregnancy and refused to let Brian have it in the house. She regaled me on the finer points of pregnancy last night on the phone."

"Oh, dear, she isn't one of those people who glories in being pregnant? You know the type, the ones that get drunk on the smell of baby powder."

"Hardly, she was thrilled to have a companion in misery. She took ghoulish pleasure in telling me the darker side of the joys of motherhood," Joanna explained with a grimace, her hand unconsciously going to her stomach. "I was starting to get used to the idea, and was almost excited about having a baby, once the shock of the doctor's confirmation had passed."

"Oh, dear."

"Don't worry, I really needed a dose of reality. Until now I'd been picturing myself as the ultimate Super Mom, sort of a combination of June Cleaver, Donna Reed, and Harriet Nelson, but in a business suit. I would do everything perfectly, because the baby wasn't going to make much of a difference in my life." She broke off as Diane burst into laughter and readily joined in at her own foolishness. "That's exactly my point. Chris brought me back down to earth and made me realize what a major change this is going to be for all of us."

"I wouldn't get too organized just yet," her friend warned her, looking at her watch before standing up. "You have a few loose ends to take care of before you start picking out nursery furniture."

"You mean like telling the father?" Joanna suggested as she got reluctantly to her feet.

"That about sums it up," Diane agreed. She took Joanna's cup and her own over to the tray by the coffee maker. "Remember, you don't have to make a decision today, but give the man a chance." With that piece of advice, she picked up the tray and left through the connecting door to her office.

The insistent buzz of the intercom didn't give Joanna any time to worry about her meeting with Nathan. She picked up the receiver and automatically said, "Yes, Anita?"

"Mr. Hartford is here, shall I show him in?"

"Yes, I'm ready." *Oh, if only I was*, she thought wildly, turning to face the doorway. Taking a deep breath, she tried to pretend that this was an ordinary appointment with an ordinary client. The only problem was she kept remembering what Nathan looked like without a stitch of clothing. It might work fine as therapy to help nervous speakers, but it didn't do a thing for her self-confidence, she decided as he walked through the door. Right now, he looked very intimidating in his charcoal gray, double breasted suit.

"Good morning, Joanna," Nathan said as he moved passed her secretary into the office. Every muscle in his body was twisted into knots. Which Joanna was he going to meet today? As he ran his gaze over her trim figure, he longed for the laughing woman who shared those carefree days on the beach in Nassau with him. The confident, remote businesswoman in front of him was a stranger.

"Hello, Nathan. Can I get you some coffee before we get started?"

He nodded, then almost jumped in surprise when she asked what he took in his coffee. *So that was how she's going to play it. She knows damn well that I take my coffee black*, he thought grimly, momentarily forgetting his own resolve to keep strictly to business. All right, two could play the game. Their personal relationship shouldn't cloud the issue. Wasn't that why he'd kept his identity a secret in Nassau? Business and pleasure were two different matters and shouldn't be mixed.

However, Joanna wasn't always going to have things her way, he decided as she walked toward him. Somehow

he was going to get back to the affair they started in
Nassau. They'd shared something special then, and he
wanted it again. He was going to get to the bottom of her
strange behavior since he'd arrived in St. Louis, one way
or the other.

"This is very impressive, Joanna. Go ahead with the
ad campaign you've planned. I can't see anything that
needs changing," Nathan said a half hour later, not giving
a damn about Hartford Consolidated or the ad campaign.
What did he care about projecting a new image west of
the Mississippi, when he was more interested in the scent
of Joanna's perfume?

"Evan said he wasn't sure about your entertainment
needs for the next few months, so I've made out a list of
alternatives that give you some flexibility," she continued
with her brisk presentation tone. "The caterer we use is
aware of our client's needs and will allow you to plan on
a short term basis, if necessary."

"Fine, Evan and I will go over our schedule and let
you know something definite as soon as possible," he
murmured, pretending to read over the list she handed
him. *What would she do if I leaned over and nibbled on
her ear?* He'd been considering it for the last fifteen
minutes as she talked about print ads and threefold
brochures.

"Nathan?"

"I'm sorry, I was thinking about a project I've been
working on," he said quickly. He had to get out of here
before he did something foolish. Torn between frustration
and admiration, he wondered how she could act as if there
was nothing more between them than an ad campaign.
She'd been friendly, though distant, never giving a hint
that they had ever made love.

"I just said, I thought we were finished," she answered
with the cool smile that he'd begun to hate.

Not by a long shot, he thought grimly, but managed a creditable smile in return. "Okay. I'll give you a call later in the week then."

"Fine."

Nathan wasn't sure what to do next. He was suppose to leave, but his feet seemed stuck to the taupe colored carpet. Staring at Joanna, he tried to think of something to say that would stretch out the moment, though he was crazy to linger. The silence between them was becoming awkward. It reminded him of the first time he'd tried to get up the nerve to kiss a girl. He'd been twelve years old, he remembered in disgust.

"Was there something else?" Joanna asked, her polite tone cutting through the stillness of the room.

"Actually, I was wondering if you were free for dinner tonight," he said rashly, almost before he realized what he was saying. From the look on Joanna's face, she was as startled as he was. He held his breath, waiting for her answer and feeling some satisfaction that he'd finally thrown her off balance.

"Oh, I'm sorry, but I already have plans."

"No problem," he said with a nonchalance he didn't feel, though he had some hope. Joanna looked as if she actually regretted having to turn him down. "Well, I'll give you a call later in the week then."

Somehow he walked out into the reception area without knowing what he was doing, or what Joanna had said before he left. *This is crazy,* he decided, stopping in the middle of the room. He was acting like a half-wit. She'd said no to one dinner invitation, and he hadn't even tried for a different night. What an idiot.

"George, this is Anita Frederico. Joanna wanted me to remind you about dinner tonight," the secretary's voice broke into his thoughts just as Nathan was about to turn around and return to Joanna's office. "I've made reservations for seven o'clock at The Inn."

Damn it, Joanna was going out with Collins tonight. Well, he wasn't going to go down without a fight, especially against Collins.

"Excuse me," he said to the secretary as she hung up the phone. He gave her his best smile, leaning over the desk near the open appointment book. "I wonder if you could recommend a nice place for dinner to a stranger in town. I couldn't help overhearing you talking about a restaurant."

"Oh, well, The Inn is a new place that's become very popular," the woman volunteered, more than willing to be of service. "It's very rustic and has a country French menu."

"That sounds just fine," he answered, his smile spreading to a confident grin. He didn't care if the place specialized in peanut butter cuisine. Joanna might not be having dinner with him, but they would be at the same restaurant. Who knew what could happen after that, especially if his aunt and uncle came along? Surely they couldn't resist saying hello to Joanna and George Collins.

Looking down at the woman's name plate on the desk, he said, "Anita, I can't tell you how much I appreciate this."

"Joanna?" Diane whispered from behind her at the same moment Nathan was strutting out of the front office, whistling under his breath.

"He's gone, if that's why you're whispering," Joanna said from where she sat slumped in the chair behind her desk. She felt like a wrung out dishrag. The last hour seemed to drag on for an eternity; every minute had been agony. But Nathan hadn't been bothered by anything, certainly not a meeting with a woman he'd slept with less than seventy-two hours ago.

"How did it go?"

"Don't get your hopes up, hon," she murmured, making the effort to sit up straight.

"Oh, Joanna."

"Don't start. I behaved myself," she shot back defensively. "I made my presentation and was friendly without being overstated."

"And?" Diane prompted as she perched on the side of the desk.

"And nothing. He was interested in the project, accomplished his business, and left," she explained, propping her chin in her hand to stare across the room. She'd been right all along. Now that he'd satisfied his male pride by bedding her again, he wasn't interested. Why couldn't he have proved her wrong?

"He just left, that's it?"

"Well, he did ask me out to dinner, only as a token gesture. When I said I had other plans, he didn't even try for another night." *Damn him.*

"Other plans? Joanna, how could you? You promised that you'd make an effort," Diane practically wailed, flexing her fists in a show of frustration.

"It's my birthday, and I'm going out to dinner with my brother, remember?" she said, almost as frustrated as Diane over the matter. However, it was a family tradition and she'd felt like Nathan was obliged to make the gesture. "I didn't tell him that I had to wash my hair instead, for heaven's sake."

"All right, this once. But the next time, you're going to cancel whatever plans you have," the blond ordered as she jumped down from the desk. "If not, I'm going to turn stool pigeon."

"If there is a next time."

* * *

"You nit wit! Did someone drop you on your head as a child?" Joanna tried to keep from yelling at George in the close confines of the car after they left the restaurant. She was still trying to recover from the shock of discovering the Hartfords at the restaurant, and Nathan's sudden change of character. And to think, only this morning, she'd been depressed by his businesslike demeanor. Ha!

"George, in heaven's name, why did you invite them back to the house?"

"It seemed like the thing to do."

"Oh, George, sometimes you amaze me," she groaned in despair. As usual he managed to remember his social graces at the wrong time. "Dinner was not my favorite experience of the year, with Nathan watching my every move from across the room. Then you decide to extend the torture for a few hours."

"I'm sorry, Jo, but Evan seemed anxious to see my pictures of the Rockies. Anyway, cheer up, Nathan's been a perfect gentleman."

That managed to silence his sister. Nathan had appeared to be the perfect gentleman to everyone else, unless they looked under the table when they'd joined the Hartfords for an after dinner drink. He'd perfected his technique since the night on the showboat, and he was now the Jacques Cousteau of foot exploration.

By subtle maneuvering, aided by Helen distracting Joanna with a question, he'd positioned himself between her and George when they sat down. The rest had been too simple. He conversed easily with the others as his foot mapped the territory of her silk covered ankle and calf. She'd nearly dropped her coffee cup with his first foray. By the time George dropped his bombshell invitation, she was ready to run screaming into the night.

As she greeted the Hartfords at George's front door

fifteen minutes later, her best company smile was in place, but the butterflies were in full flight in the pit of her stomach. What caused the change in Nathan from earlier today? It couldn't be because of George, though he'd acted jealous of her brother that first night at the Hartford party. She'd never understand the man, or figure out how he got his shoe off and on tonight without anyone noticing.

"If you'll excuse me for a minute, I'll go start the coffee," she announced after everyone was settled and George began setting up the projector.

"Wait a second, Joanna, I have something I was going to announce tomorrow, but I think I'll go ahead and jump the gun." Evan's words stopped her in mid stride. When she glanced in question at her brother, he shrugged to show he was as bewildered as she was.

"I'd like to present our newest field supervisor, George Collins. At least he will be officially as soon as the Washington project is finished," Evan explained, giving the younger man a hardy slap on the back.

"I'm speechless," George finally managed after swallowing several times. He didn't seem to know what to do next, fiddling with the projector cord.

"Nonsense, my boy," Evan stated, "it should have been done before we took over. We can't have you hidden away in the design room, especially now that you're thinking about settling down."

"Yes, sir," George said happily as he hugged his sister, oblivious to Evan's not so subtle hint about his relationship with Joanna, "and you couldn't have picked a better night. It's Joanna's birthday."

"Birthday, how old are you, dear? Certainly not old enough for you to lie about it yet," Helen accused Joanna when she didn't answer immediately. The older woman hadn't seen the frown that creased Nathan's face a few minutes before.

"Thirty," Joanna murmured, wishing George hadn't mentioned it. A single, direct look from Nathan's gray eyes reminded her of the last conversation she'd had about her age.

"How old are you?" Nathan had asked unexpectedly that first night in Nassau over dinner. "This afternoon on the float I'd have guessed very early twenties, but now that halter dress certainly does something for you, as well as for me."

"Oh, you're being kind. I'm twenty-nine." She'd smiled at his smooth approach, subtly trying to undermine any resistance by playing on her vanity.

"Good, that removes any feelings of guilt I might have had." He raised his glass to hers, his challenging slanted smile sending a fision of anticipation down her bare back.

"Why guilt?"

"The gap between twenty and thirty-five might have kept me awake at night, but a five year difference assures me of pleasant dreams instead."

"What exactly did you have in mind with only a five year difference?" She'd known the answer, but wanted to see how he would explain it.

"Why companionship, of course," he'd answered innocently, trying to look outraged that she would think of any other reason.

"Well, that closes the gap to four years," Nathan murmured as he stood beside her for a moment, ready to shake hands with George.

"It's nothing for you to lose any sleep over," Joanna retorted sweetly before she realized her poor choice of words.

"I don't plan to, I told you that," was Nathan's even reply before he returned to his chair.

Joanna was saved from answering by Evan's next question. "So, George, have you made any definite plans about getting married? You'll have some free time at the end of this project."

She wanted to sink into the floor. This was not the life line she was looking for. And George didn't help matters.

"That's right, I will," he managed weakly, looking at his sister for support, almost willing her to do something that would rescue him. His baffled expression clearly told her he had no idea how he'd gotten into this predicament. He'd forgotten about pretending she was his date at the Hartford party.

Perversely, she decided that he could twist his way out of this dilemma by himself. "I think I'll go get the coffee started. Would anyone prefer tea instead?"

When no one spoke up, she headed for the kitchen, waving in response to George's reminder to check the white bakery box on the counter.

"This is a nice old house, very comfortable," a deep voice interrupted her a few minutes later as she foraged in the refrigerator. "You seem to know your way around fairly well."

Joanna straightened hastily and twisted around, clutching the refrigerator door to keep her balance. Nathan stood in the center of the room, his feet slightly apart and his hands thrust into his pockets. He'd taken off his jacket and loosened his tie. She could almost imagine they were in their own kitchen.

"Sorry, I didn't mean to startle you. I thought you heard the door squeak," he said too nicely, leaving Joanna to doubt his sincerity. "I only came in to see if I could help carry anything."

She acknowledged his offer with a nod before turning her attention to the tray by the sink. Efficiently she cut the birthday cake George had unexpectedly provided and arranged the plates. Let Nathan handle the conversation, she thought recklessly. If necessary, she could leave the room.

"I take it you've known Collins a long time," he observed casually, his tone a study in nonchalance.

"Yes," she said succinctly, wondering what he was going to do now. He had her confused and nervous with his abrupt personality changes, but damned if she was going to let him know that. And if he hadn't discovered George was her brother yet, she wasn't going to be the one to enlighten him. Trying to get the lid off the non-dairy creamer was a handy diversion.

"Here let me," Nathan murmured close to her ear, too close for him to still be leaning against the counter across the room. She froze, staring forward and refusing to give in to the need to see exactly where he was. Then his hand appeared in her line of vision, plucking the jar from her unresisting hand. His other hand came down on her shoulder for a moment.

She watched in rapt fascination as he gave the lid a quick twist, opening it effortlessly. When she reached for the jar, he didn't relax his hold, forcing her to look at him. His gray eyes seemed to be searching for something in her expression. "Is Collins the reason you've changed since I came to St. Louis?"

"I haven't changed," she answered honestly, unable to move or look away. "Nassau was a fantasy, a temporary and dangerous apparition." *More dangerous than I knew*, she thought wildly as he drew a caressing finger down her cheek. "I went a little crazy for a few days. Now I'm back to the real world where everything is exactly as it's supposed to be. There's no pretense, no lies."

"What lies?" He actually looked bewildered by her words for a minute before his expression became guarded. His eyes narrowed as he cocked his head to the side, waiting for her explanation.

"Your lies of omission, Nathan," she said clearly, unconsciously raising her chin with the accusation. The warmth of his body and the spicy smell of his aftershave were bringing back too many memories. She was beginning to feel trapped between him and the counter. "You knew exactly who I was from the minute we met, but you had to play your little game. Is that a standard means of seduction for you, keeping your identity a secret?"

"So that's it. Joanna, listen to me," he put down the jar impatiently, the glass hitting the linoleum with a loud slap. His hands closed over her shoulders, as though he was afraid she'd turn away.

She wasn't going to let him work his charm on her again. Though she agreed to become better acquainted with the man, she wasn't going to become ensnared by his charm again. "Nathan, there isn't anything you can say about Nassau that I want to hear. It's history, finished. We are business associates, nothing more."

"That's exactly why I didn't tell you who I was. Business wasn't exactly my first priority."

He gave her an entreating look, but she was so confused at this point she didn't know what to say or do. Not letting her gaze drop, she took a deep breath. "Nathan, this isn't the time or the place to discuss the matter. Just let it drop."

"That wasn't what you were telling me the other night or when we were in Nassau. There is something special between us, it's been there since the day we met. If you hadn't run out on me, you wouldn't be considering a relationship with Collins now."

Her resistance was waning, and she hated herself for wanting to give in. It wasn't fair. She was still trying to cope with the discovery of her pregnancy and wasn't ready to attempt sorting out her conflicting emotions toward Nathan as well.

"I don't trust you, Nathan." Her voice came out as a whisper of sound, barely able to form the words.

His tentative smile faded and two lines creased his forehead as his brows drew together. As his fingers pressed into her shoulders she wondered if he was going to shake her, or pull her into his arms. She couldn't read his expression, but she knew he wasn't complacent about their relationship. Whatever his motives were in Nassau, it was becoming clear they had nothing to do with business. She was torn between relief at the discovery and panic at what it meant.

Whatever Nathan intended was interrupted by the warning squeak of the kitchen door. By the time Evan entered the kitchen, the couple was three feet apart, watching each other warily.

"I thought I'd see if everything was all right," he said, giving them an inquiring look.

Joanna picked up the tray, looking directly at Evan with a bright, painful, smile. "Oh, yes. I've put Nathan in charge of the coffee, so I'm ready to join the rest of you in the living room. I haven't had a chance to see George's slides myself."

Evan watched her flounce through the door while Nathan stared at the coffee maker as if it were an alien life form. A slight smile appeared on his face as he sauntered toward his nephew.

"It's not so hard to figure out, the water goes in the top and the coffee goes in the little basket do-hicky, not nearly as complicated as the workings of a woman's mind," he said quietly, before turning to leave without another word.

A very confused man stayed behind, cursing at the hapless appliance.

SIX

"Joanna, I really feel silly," Diane complained from the passenger seat the next evening for the third time in as many miles.

"Oh, for heaven's sake, not again," she moaned as she stopped the car for a red light. "There's nothing silly about coming with me to George's house. It isn't as if it's the first time."

"I didn't have any ulterior motives for my visits before tonight," the blond protested next to her, red staining her fair complexion.

Joanna was amused and relieved by her friend's agitation. As long as Diane fretted over her brother, there wouldn't be any uncomfortable questions about the state of her own affairs. She didn't want to talk about Nathan because she still hadn't come up with a viable plan. Scarlett O'Hara had the right idea; tomorrow was a much better alternative.

"None that you admitted to at the time," Joanna added without rancor. "I can't believe these feelings simply cropped up over night. So, give me the story."

"I guess it started at Brian's birthday party, when George tripped and spilled his drink on my dress," Diane admitted, a sheepish smile curving her lips.

"Typical."

"After I went home to change, he showed up at my apartment," she continued as if Joanna hadn't said a word. "He was really upset about the whole mess and wanted to pay the cleaning bill."

"You're kidding?" His sister gasped in surprise before she could help herself and was rewarded with a glare.

"He was genuinely upset, so I asked him to stay for coffee. I think that was the first time in three years that I ever talked to him outside of hello-how-are-you.

"When you came down with the flu, we seemed to be thrown together," she continued while Joanna was preoccupied with the traffic. "You know, he'd pick up work from the office, or I'd run into him at your place. The more I saw him, the more I liked him." She broke off with a small sigh, then forged ahead once more. "Then one day he stopped by on an errand for you, and we had lunch together."

"You can't stop there," Joanna exclaimed when it seemed that Diane wasn't going to say another word.

"Well, I can't explain this so it will sound rational," she explained hesitantly. "We were sitting there talking, just waiting for our food. I don't understand what happened myself. Something he said or did just hit me. That's the best I can do. It barely took a minute, but suddenly I realized I was crazy about him. Amazing, isn't it?"

"Not as amazing as you think," Joanna murmured as she turned the car into her brother's driveway. Maybe she would have found it incredible a few months ago, before Nassau. Now it sounded so nice and comfortable, the right way to fall in love. As she climbed out of the car, she discovered that she envied her friend's uncomplicated story.

"Hey, I thought you'd be here a half hour ago,"

George yelled from where he leaned on the railing of the front porch, pulling Joanna back to the present.

"I got caught in traffic on the way home from work and got home late," she called back. "Then Diane came over, so I brought her along."

"Whoops. If I'd known I was having real company I'd have dressed better," he answered, indicating his paint spattered cut-offs and dark green T-shirt with an anxious look.

"Don't panic, hon," Diane told him, flashing her brightest smile. "I'll close my eyes and conjure up that suit you had on at the Hartford shindig. Only one problem, what color was it?"

"Beats me. I'll have to drop by the office in a tux later in the week to dazzle everyone."

"You do that," Diane shot back as they walked into the house. "I'm getting bored with having lunch with Joanna all the time. A new face is always welcome."

"Thanks a lot," Joanna grumbled good-naturedly while she silently admired her friend's technique. Fleetingly she wondered if she shouldn't get some coaching from the woman. It certainly couldn't hurt. She hadn't done very well in her last few encounters with Nathan.

"My dear Joanna, you may have the family looks," her brother explained with an exaggerated drawl, "but when it comes to charm they knew who would put it to the best use."

Joanna groaned and stuck her finger in her mouth in a gesture from her childhood. "I think I'll make a hasty retreat to the basement and put a final coat of wax on my table." As she headed for the basement steps she casually called over her shoulder, "Why don't you show Diane around the house, that way she won't be bored to tears watching me."

A half hour later she came back upstairs to find George expounding on the intricacies of his new sound system to an enthralled Diane. She watched in amusement as he absentmindedly draped his arm over the blond's shoulder to draw her attention to one particular feature. Perhaps Diane wasn't going to have to work too hard on getting his attention after all.

Rather than break into the conversation, she picked up a magazine and settled into the nearest chair to pass the time. There wasn't any way to gauge when George or Diane would remember her presence. Her peaceful occupation was disrupted, however, by the strident ring of the phone on the end table next to her.

She reached for the receiver on reflex. "Collins residence."

"How are you, Joanna?"

"Fine, and you?" she asked as her body involuntarily responded to Nathan's deep, lazy voice. Damn, why had she answered the phone?

"I'm not interrupting anything, am I?" he asked, his inflection causing her hand to tighten around the receiver.

"I won't lose my place," she responded quickly, looking down at the magazine on her lap. She smiled slightly as she realized that her mind worked clearly when she wasn't distracted by Nathan's disturbing body. "George can't come to the phone right now, can I take a message?"

"If he can find the time this evening, I'd like the figures on the Washington project first thing in the morning." The words were terse, as if Nathan might be losing some of his usual composure.

"Why certainly, I'd be glad to tell him. Is there anything else I can do for you?" she asked politely, ready to hang up as soon as he said good-bye.

"Yes, as a matter of fact there is," he returned smoothly, jolting her out of her complacency. The phone wasn't so safe after all. "When can we finish last night's conversation? We were interrupted at a very interesting point, and you managed to keep at least half the room between us the rest of the night.''

Joanna closed her eyes, trying to think of a sophisticated, witty reply. Nothing came to her as her heart beat accelerated and her hands began to sweat. She resorted to panic.

''I really can't talk right now,'' she blurted out and quickly dropped the receiver into its cradle. For a moment she sat with her body clenched in almost a fetal position wondering if the phone would ring again. What had happened to her usual steady nerves? She was always the calm one in every situation.

''Well?'' George asked from across the room. Joanna opened her eyes to find both her brother and Diane watching her with puzzled expressions over her strange behavior. ''That was for me, wasn't it?''

''Yes, it was your boss. He wants the figures for your big project tomorrow first thing.''

''From the tone of the conversation, I take it that was Nathan,'' Diane commented as she sat down in the rocker across from Joanna. Her disapproving frown made Joanna shift uneasily in her chair.

''I don't get it,'' George exclaimed when Joanna nodded. He reached up to scratch the back of his head in a characteristic thinking gesture. ''What is this nonsense between you and Nathan? You begin acting bizarre the minute he appears. Last night you were like a hyperactive kid, jumping all over the living room whenever he made a move or cleared his throat.''

''Jo, you didn't tell me you'd seen Nat—''

''It's just bad chemistry, I guess.'' Joanna broke ruthlessly into Diane's accusation. George didn't know anything more than her meeting with Nathan while on vacation. Now wasn't the time to bring him up to date or tell him about his impending unclehood. That was one decision she had made. She was going to tell the father before she told anyone else about her baby.

"Isn't there any way you can manage to at least be civil to the guy?" he asked in exasperation, dropping into the nearest chair and propping his arms on his thighs.

"George, I think you're being a little rough on her," Diane intervened, intercepting a desperate look from Joanna. She hesitated as Joanna pointed to her stomach and shook her head vigorously. Diane nodded in comprehension and continued. "Nathan isn't an angel, especially after last week. He must own a florist shop by now."

"Hold it a minute, you've lost me," George said, looking back and forth between the two women, more confused than before Diane's comments. "What does a florist have to do with this?"

"Didn't she tell you about the flowers he sent?"

"Joanna?"

"Here we go again. I didn't mention it because you were out of town." She squirmed slightly under her brother's accusing glare. Why did George have to pick now to be fairly lucid? "He simply sent me flowers every day while he was in Chicago."

"That's *all!*" George exploded out of his chair, and began pacing the floor. "I don't think I like this at all. Are you sure you told me everything about your first meeting in Nassau?"

"Yes, positive," Joanna mumbled, hiding her crossed fingers behind her back as she refused to meet Diane's startled look. It was the truth; she hadn't found out she was pregnant until two months after her trip.

"I don't buy that, but I suppose it's not going to do any good to argue," he muttered as he sat down again. Massaging his jaw reflectively, he studied his sister. "Just promise me one thing."

"That depends on what it is."

"Don't go out of your way to antagonize Nathan any more than you have to, please? I would really like to keep my job."

"I won't promise because I don't think Nathan's the type of man to fire someone over a personal matter. However, I will try to be as pleasant as possible the next time I see him," she told him with a simpering smile. *Unfortunately, I think that will be too soon for my peace of mind*, she decided as Diane cleared her throat. She knew the other woman was reminding her of another promise she'd made about Nathan. Running away to a secluded cave to be a hermit was becoming an attractive idea.

George threw his hands up in despair, and turned to Diane. "How about having that lunch tomorrow? I need some answers, and you're the only one here who won't start weaving fairy tales the minute I open my mouth."

"Why not?" Diane sat back in her chair with a complacent smile across her face. Joanna's grimace and surreptitious hand gestures couldn't erase her dreamy expression.

When the alarm woke her the next morning Joanna didn't need to look out the window at the overcast skies to know the day ahead would be dismal. The tension headache she'd developed over the past few days was still lingering as a dull ache. Her morning sickness seemed to escalate as well. She'd slept fitfully, dreaming a disjointed mixture of palm trees, baby strollers, and an army of smiling men with mustaches. Listlessly she dressed for work, knowing that she'd have to make a decision about talking to Nathan by the end of the week.

As she walked back to the office at lunch time her appetite had returned, but she had about as much energy as Raggedy Ann. The prim receptionist at her last appointment kept giving her disapproving looks as Joanna waited for her appointment with her head tilted back against the back of the couch with her eyes closed. She wondered what the woman would have done if she'd proclaimed that she was an unwed mother, who was suffering from pregnancy, not a hangover.

"Is it a private joke, or can you share it?" Brian Judson's voice broke into her musings at the moment she pictured the woman's horrified expression with satisfaction.

"Hello, where did you spring from?"

"How observant you are, spider legs." He chuckled at her disgusted look over her childhood nickname, shoving his hands in the trouser pockets of his pin-striped suit. "I've been following you for about two blocks, but you were lost in your own world."

"I must be slipping, but not enough to let you get away with calling me that hideous name," she stated, shaking an admonishing finger at his unrepentant grin. "Honestly, Brian, you know I never liked it. You should be careful, or I might remember a few myself."

"In that case, I'll treat you to lunch," he asserted, trying to repress his amusement and look suitably chasten. "Not because of my philanthropic nature, it'll be a bribe."

"Done. Where to?" She hadn't been looking forward to eating a carry-out sandwich at her desk. Lunch with an old friend who wouldn't discuss prenatal care or a certain gentleman was just the anecdote she needed today.

"How about my favorite delicatessen?" he asked as he took her arm and started down the street. "I'm meeting a client there in about a half hour."

"The deli sounds heavenly. I'll drown my sorrows in an enormous piece of cheese cake, in spite of what it might do to my waist line." *It's going to be shot to flinders fairly soon anyway, and dairy products were probably good for the baby*. As they walked to the restaurant, she remembered she needed to pick up some books on prenatal care and nutrition.

"Now, what's this about drowning your sorrows?" Brian asked after they'd gone through the line and found a quiet, corner table amid the other diners.

Joanna hesitated for a moment, biting into her pastrami sandwich as a delaying tactic. Though she hadn't told Chris not to tell Brian about the baby, she was relieved that he didn't seem to know. She'd be cautious, however, until she was sure. "Are you going to be my confessor again? Didn't you retire from the advice business when you graduated from high school?"

"I got you through puberty, didn't I? What's your nitwit brother done now?"

"Actually George has been on his good behavior lately, so there," she shot back, wiping the cole slaw dressing that dripped from her sandwich from her fingers. Brian had always been impatient with George's absentmindedness that somehow embroiled Joanna in his mishaps.

"Amazing."

"I'll pretend I didn't hear that," she murmured around another bite of sandwich.

"Then it must be a certain someone that my wife has been babbling about lately," he declared with an expectant look. "If I wasn't so secure in my masculinity, I'd be jealous."

"What do you mean?" She froze in her seat, ignoring his facetious comment. Maybe Chris had told him.

"As if you didn't know."

"Give me a hint," she hedged, holding her breath for his next words. *Please, please, be talking about someone else, don't say the N-word.*

"Oh, how sweet and innocent you've become," he challenged. "I saw how Nathan looked at you that night at my house. I'm not a complete idiot."

"The jury is still out on the latter," she murmured as she played for time. *Of course he was talking about Nathan, wasn't everybody?* "And the gentleman isn't my favorite subject right now." How was she ever going to come to a rational decision about the man if everyone kept throwing him at her? The more they pushed, the more resistant she became, whether it was logical or not. Her apartment was becoming the only place she seemed to be safe from the mention of his name. Though he'd already made inroads there as well.

"What's the matter, Jo, won't he let you have your own way?" he teased, the wicked gleam in his eyes was one Joanna knew to distrust from years of experience.

"Very funny. I'm simply tired of hearing about him. If it isn't George singing his praises, it's dealing with Hartford's erratic schedule at work." She paused to take a deep swallow of lemonade. Prevarication was thirsty work. "I'm beginning to think it's all part of a conspiracy."

"Only this time," Brian said softly, glancing over her shoulder toward the deli counter. "I forgot to mention the name of the client I was meeting today."

"Oh, Brian, no," she groaned, horrified as she swung around to see Nathan weaving his way toward them between the crowded tables.

She felt as though she was trapped in an old stockbroker ad. Nathan seemed to be approaching in slow motion while, to Joanna's frenetic imagination, everyone in the restaurant fell silent, waiting for her to react. She could almost hear the somber voice of the announcer intoning, *Will she jump to her feet and proclaim her condition to the entire room of strangers, or simply plunge her plastic fork into the man's heart?*

"Hello, Nathan," she managed in a fairly creditable

voice, accompanied by a tight smile as she relaxed her hold on her fork.

Her mind was working feverishly to find a means of escape, when, of course, there wasn't one. However, her pride wouldn't let either man know her true feelings. *Stay calm, Joanna. You can handle this. Just make some idle conversation for a few minutes, excuse yourself, and run like hell, just as fast as your cowardly legs can carry you.*

Nodding at Brian, he gave her a wary look as he sat in the empty chair next to her. "I didn't know you would be joining us today."

"Yes, it is a surprise, isn't it?" she agreed, her voice bright and cheerful as she glared at Brian, who had remained silent after greeting the other man.

"I knew it couldn't be the thought of seeing me again so soon," Nathan said in a monotone, watching her from beneath half closed eyelids.

Joanna's harassed mind couldn't think of a quick retort, so she continued to smile as sweetly as possible. Then she took refuge behind her lemonade glass as Nathan continued to watch her speculatively. Looking over the rim, she realized Brian was taking in the exchange with a somewhat satisfied expression, before his twinkling glance met her malevolent look.

"Well, Nathan, I think we're ready to go ahead," Brian broke into speech after clearing his throat. Unconsciously, he adjusted his tie. "Chris and I took number one son out for a visit to look over the property this weekend."

"And?" the other man asked anxiously, a smile of anticipation slanting his moustache to the side.

"It's ideal for the house you have in mind."

"House?" Joanna jumped at the mention of the word. Her mind really was beginning to atrophy. Why else would Nathan be consulting Brian? "Is Brian designing a house for you?"

"Why naturally, since he's the only architect I know personally. I can't see spending my life in a hotel suite, or paying exorbitant rent for an indefinite period of time," Nathan responded quickly, seeming to be fascinated by her consternation. "I think it's time I set up a permanent home base."

"What did you do in Philadelphia?" Joanna inquired in spite of herself. There was so much about this man that she didn't know. Though she knew she should leave, she wanted to know about his house.

"I renovated the coach house at my parents' house. Since I was rarely at home it seemed the best plan. Now I won't be traveling as much and can finally put down some roots."

"You just send other people away instead," Joanna murmured without realizing she'd spoken aloud.

"You can't expect me to do every project myself. You must have realized that George would have to travel in his job eventually."

She shrugged for want of a better answer. Using George as a red herring in front of Brian was too chancy.

"You should have made better use of your time together when George was in town, Joanna," Brian interrupted, entirely too quick on the uptake for her peace of mind. The man had a perverse sense of humor to tease her this way.

She could feel the flush of anger staining her cheeks at the flagrant advantage Brian was taking of the situation. Biting back a scathing reply, she decided now was the time for retreat. "I really should be getting back to the office."

"Oh, no, Joanna. I really think we could use a woman's opinion on some of these plans. Don't you, Nathan?" Brian busied himself with pulling the blue print from the leather case at his side.

"If you wouldn't mind."

Although she didn't understand why, Joanna relaxed in her chair. It couldn't have been the entreating look that momentarily flashed in Nathan's gray eyes. She was simply curious about what type of house he'd want to build, then regretted the inquisitive impulse almost immediately. The Dutch colonial was a fantasy come true as far as she was concerned, from its dormer windows to the stone fireplace. After fifteen minutes of torturing herself, she decided to try for freedom again, waiting patiently for an opening in the discussion.

"I really should charge you for aggravation pay, since I have an expectant mother to humor thanks to you," Brian stated, unaware of the conversation time bomb he was handling. "Chris is starting to talk about renovations, now that she's seen that utility island and pantry we've planned."

"How's she doing? Last time I talked to her she was threatening to hang you up by your thumbs, but she didn't have time to explain why," Nathan said with a polite smile, though his eyes kept wandering to Joanna.

"She's not usually so violent, only on odd Tuesdays," her husband explained affectionately. "I brought home a pizza that night, unaware that the smell didn't exactly agree with her. With Jeffrey, she couldn't tolerate coffee, but when a woman's expecting you never know what's going to go wrong next. She actually cried over a broken iron yesterday, even when I promised to go out immediately and buy a new one."

Joanna wanted to slide under the table. How could she anticipate Brian gossiping about his wife's pregnancy? She clenched her hands under the table, trying to remain as still as possible, barely daring to breath. What evil quirk in her mind had earlier told her to stay?

"Did it work?" Nathan asked with fascinated interest.

"Are you kidding? It only made her cry harder, then Jeffrey started in sympathy for his mother," Brian said, giving Nathan one of those male looks of superior intelligence. "There's no telling what she'll react to next. Just yesterday morning she was craving bacon, then ran out of the room before she took a bite. If I didn't know better, I'd suspect it was revenge for the next seven months."

"Before you get in trouble, I think I'll head back to work," Joanna broke in, relieved at the chance to make a reasonable exit. She felt like a neon sign was suddenly flashing, *Baby on Board* across her chest, an arrow pointing toward her abdomen. "I don't think you want a woman around for the rest of this conversation."

"Oh, boy. Should I open my mouth and insert the other foot?" Brian gave her his best boyish smile, then pretended to be wounded by her disdainful look.

"Before you go, Joanna, I have a favor to ask," Nathan said quickly, getting to his feet. He hesitated for a moment, reaching up to stroke his moustache in an unconscious gesture.

Joanna took an involuntary step back, wondering what he could be thinking. Now what? Hadn't the last half hour been nerve wracking enough? "What is it, Nathan?"

"Brian was right about the need for a woman's opinion. So, I was wondering if you'd like to go out and see the property this weekend." The words came out in a rush as he stuck his hands in his pockets, his face intent as he waited for her answer.

She didn't know what to say for a moment, or if she could even speak if she tried. This wasn't what she expected, but she knew she would have to accept. She couldn't refuse in front of Brian without looking churlish. Just this morning, Diane had threatened to do something drastic if Joanna didn't attempt to contact Nathan soon, especially after last night's phone call at George's house. She had to face the problem, whether she liked it or not.

"All right," she finally managed, her fingers fidgeting with the handle of her briefcase. "Why don't I make a picnic lunch to take along?" *Good heavens, where did that come from?* she wondered wildly as she waited for his answer.

The transformation in Nathan was incredible. A grin flashed into place as he straightened his shoulders. "That's a great idea. I'll give you a call tomorrow to set up a time."

"Fine," she mumbled, then with a nod at Brian, she turned on her heel and fled. She was afraid to stay a minute longer in case she did something else on impulse. First she'd agreed to spend time with Nathan, and capped that amazing feat by turning domestic. Pregnancy was doing some very strange things to her mind.

Nathan watched Joanna's retreating figure until she was out of sight, unaware that he was still standing. A man at the next table jostled him when he pushed back his chair, and Nathan realized what he was doing. He sat down quickly, and concentrated on his food, all too aware of Brian's considering look. He let the silence lengthen, savoring the small kernel of anticipation, and relief, that curled inside him at Joanna's unexpected acceptance.

"Well, at least you didn't strike out; that's real progress," Brian finally commented, his lips twitching with suppressed laughter as the other man looked up, feigning surprise. "So, what's so exciting about that sandwich?"

"That is one unpredictable lady," Nathan answered, giving up the pretense he didn't understand the other man. They had already spent too many hours together while planning his house. He not only liked Brian, he trusted him.

"You can say that again, but you haven't seen anything

yet," Brian stated with the superiority of a married man. After a moment's consideration he allowed himself a small chuckle. "This has been a very enlightening lunch." He paused for a minute, making a great effort to scrape up the last of his potato salad from his plate.

"You're a sadist, Judson. Why has it been enlightening?"

"I've never seen anyone get to Joanna that way. One minute she's furious you're here, then she's offering to make your lunch."

"That's good?" Nathan was totally confused, beginning to wonder if he was the last sane person in St. Louis.

"Well, it's good and bad," Brian reassured him, clearing the perplexed expression from his friend's face. "Joanna is usually one of the most controlled people I know, especially with people she hasn't known very long. She prides herself on being logical, practical, and organized. Usually she keeps her feelings inside, never really showing her true emotions. Whenever you're around, she's always off balance."

"That's the good part, right? So, what's the bad part?"

"Joanna doesn't cook very often, so you'd better hope she doesn't fix that picnic herself."

"Damn, I wish I knew if you were serious or not," Nathan muttered. The lady was enigmatic, so he didn't need more cryptic comments from his friends. "I think the next time your wife threatens you, I'll volunteer to help."

"I'm serious about the whole thing," Brian assured him, giving his friend a measuring look, almost sizing him up. "You just keep her worked up and things should progress nicely. It's when she's cool and calm that you should start to worry."

"So, the more she squirms, the better I'm doing? And here I thought I was doing so well when she agreed to see me on Saturday without any coercion." Nathan chuckled over this absurd logic. Then another problem came to mind. "What about Collins?"

"Oh, I wouldn't lose any sleep over Joanna and George. Their relationship is strictly platonic," Brian instructed, knowing he could be in serious trouble for this piece of advice. "You just concentrate on Joanna."

"Well, let's hope my luck continues, and I can keep her agitated." Though he tried to remain nonchalant in front of Brian, he wanted to get up and shout at the top of his lungs. He'd finally made some progress, and it had been an impulsive, unvarnished invitation that had done it. Now all he had to do was keep from screwing things up again on Saturday with his impatience. His track record wasn't very good so far, but with each passing day he knew he had to have Joanna in his life.

"Are you taking up transcendental meditation by any chance?" Diane's voice broke through Joanna's consciousness as she sat behind her desk staring into space.

"Not exactly. I was trying to solve the mystique of the American male," Joanna returned, still grappling with accepting Nathan's invitation, then gave an exaggerated shrug. Though she knew she had to begin acting like a rational adult again, she was scared spitless. "It's as twisted as a Rubic's Cube." She put up a hand at Diane's raised eyebrows. There wasn't any way she could explain what had happened at lunch when she didn't understand it herself. "Don't ask. What did you need?"

"We have a major SNAFU," the blond admitted, looking crestfallen at not hearing about whatever was bothering Joanna.

"Something new, or the same old problems?" Joanna was ready for any diversion. She had plenty of time for her nervous breakdown before Saturday.

"A new one. What are your plans this weekend?"

Joanna didn't believe she'd heard correctly at first, but wanted to remain noncommittal. "Nothing terribly pressing," she answered slowly, almost afraid to hear what Diane had to say. "Why?"

"Fred was going to check out the larger cabin down at Lake of the Ozarks," Diane explained as she perched in her usual place at the side of the desk. "Bert Tracy called about a new place with four bedrooms while you were on vacation."

"So what's the problem?"

"Fred can't drive with a broken collar bone, dummy, and his wife doesn't drive at all, remember?" Diane chided gently. "I have to go down to Cape Girardeau for a sorority reunion Saturday afternoon."

"So I'm elected," Joanna murmured, ignoring the wave of disappointment that suddenly washed over her. She should be jumping for joy; it was the perfect excuse to cancel the picnic.

"Right, you're it, because my assistant hasn't been with us long enough for this type of appraisal. Bert says he'll have all the power turned on and the phone connected by Friday night. He'll also check the food supplies."

"What's this one like? Not another nightmare?" she asked, her mind turning completely to business. When Diane had the inspiration of supplying a place for weekend meetings, there had been a limited selection. Danish modern furnishing and aluminum siding didn't exactly coordinate in her mind with a wooded lakeside retreat.

"Bert sent pictures along this time. It's a beaut. Real log timbers and Early American furnishings," Diane began passing the photographs across the desk as she continued her enthusiastic description. "There are four bedrooms, two baths, and a gorgeous stone fireplace in the living room. What do you think?"

"It's terrific," Joanna said in awe as she shuffled through the photographs. "Who owns this place, and is crazy enough to let it go?"

"No, a history professor with extremely good taste," Diane clarified. "He's going overseas for two years and is willing to rent to the right people. Harvey Longnecker at Johnson Manufacturing suggested he call us."

"It sounds too good to be true," Joanna stated, knowing there wasn't any way to schedule another visit. This had to be her first priority. So why wasn't she overjoyed that she wouldn't be seeing Nathan? "We'd better grab it. The same arrangements as before?"

"We pay a flat rate, and Bert rents it out when we aren't scheduled, which won't be very often now that we have the larger accommodations. We'll also take over the insurance payments."

"Great, I'll go down Friday afternoon and come back Sunday night," Joanna decided. "That will give me two blissful days to myself. The lake is an ideal place to work out what I'm going to do in the next seven months, and afterward."

When Diane left, Joanna sat staring at the telephone, reluctant to make the necessary call. Would he believe that a business problem had come up over the weekend? Or would he think she was making another excuse to avoid him?

Before she could change her mind, she reached for the phone, amazed at the irony of the situation. After two weeks of playing cat and mouse with the man, she was sorry that she had to cancel their plans. Life just didn't make sense at times.

A minute later she slapped the receiver back in place. Naturally he wasn't in the office after she'd braced herself to face his questions. How long was she going to be on tenterhooks wondering when he would return her call?

SEVEN

"You picked a hell of a day for a drive, missy," Bert Tracy called to Joanna as she waited for him to walk up the dock behind his rental store.

"Don't I know it," she answered as she waited for the lanky man to join her, still flexing her stiff shoulder muscles. After almost an entire week of glorious spring sunshine, it turned threatening and overcast for her drive to the cabin. She'd made it halfway here before the deluge began, but the rain had stopped about a half hour ago. The only advantage to the weather was not having a chance to think of anything but driving.

"Have you been here long? I've been working out in the boat house gettin' things set for the summer season," Bert announced, glancing up at the darkening sky as he reached her side. Not waiting for her to respond, he wiped his hands on the kerchief in the back pocket of his work pants, then offered her his hand. "Good to see you again. We'd better get you settled in, 'cause I think it's fixin' to start again any minute."

"I think you're right," she agreed and trotted up the wooden steps to the back of the store. Bert kept a fleet of motor boats and stocked just about everything in the double size log cabin that was necessary for a day on the lake from fishing tackle to water skis. Tracy's Store was the place for supplies and gossip since Bert and his wife Celia knew everything and everyone for miles around.

"You're goin' to love Sid's place, calls it a cabin, but between you and me, I call it a house." Bert kept talking without bothering to see if Joanna kept up with his long legged strides. "I went down this mornin' to check the electricity and water. The phone hasn't been disconnected either, and Celia made sure there's enough food for an army. That woman thinks everyone eats like our boys, so you won't go hungry."

"I really appreciate your help with this, Bert. If this works out you're going to have lots of Trent-Barringer customers on your doorstep." She watched in fascination as he shuffled through a mountain of papers on the battered roll top desk. Bert was a true character, and he made a study of it, dressing and speaking the part. Joanna knew that he was a retired English professor from the university in Springfield, and he had the time of his life playing boat mechanic for the summer folks.

"That's exactly why I made sure I'd find you a good location. I've got two kids in college and another one about ready," Bert said with a wink, then gave a grunt of satisfaction as he found what he was looking for in one of the cubby holes. The keys to the cabin. "If I can't swing this deal, Celia might have to take in laundry to make ends meet."

"You're a big fraud, Bert," she answered, grinning at his foolishness. The Tracys could buy and sell half the state of Missouri.

"Don't you tell anybody. It'd be bad for business," he ordered, but he couldn't maintain his fierce scowl of reproof for long. He broke into his lazy smile, and told her, "You holler if you need anything. There's only two or three people in residence right now. Just head down the road a half mile and take the first turn off to the right. Now skedaddle before you get soaked.''

"All right, I'll see you and Celia on Sunday before I leave." Joanna gave him a smart salute before she headed for the car. Bert wasn't kidding. The wind had picked up and the clouds looked ready to burst their seams as she turned the car down the road. Ten minutes later as the car wheels crunched along the gravel road that led to the cabin, she hoped she would make it inside where it would be safe and warm before the next downpour.

The skies were still threatening as she pulled into the yard in front of the stone and wood house. Not wanting to tempt fate, she prepared to run from the car with more speed than grace. Her suitcase in one hand and groping for the key in her pocket with the other, Joanna trotted up the grassy slope to the front door.

One minute she was laughing in triumph as her hand closed over the key chain, the next she was swearing heatedly, lying on the ground. Her face was a mere inch from the patch of mud she'd slipped on. Scrambling to her feet as quickly as the wet surface of the grass under her rubber soles would allow, she surveyed the damage.

Her chest was dark, mud brown, no longer the tangerine and yellow of her T-shirt and windbreaker. She'd managed to escape the full force of her fall from the waist down. Her jeans and track shoes were only lightly splattered with the brown goo. Luckily her suitcase was thrown clear, landing in the thick grass a few feet away. She picked it up, stomping to the door, and becoming more disgusted at every step as the mud slipped down under the neckline of her shirt.

Once inside she pushed off her shoes and reversed her jacket, using it to cover the mess on her chest to keep from dripping on the braid rug. She headed for the master bedroom with one purpose in mind—a long, hot shower. Five minutes later she stripped off her messy clothes and stepped under the steamy spray. Outside, a threatening rumble of thunder announced the beginning of the rain storm.

After a few minutes Joanna felt revived as the warm water coursed over her back. She shut off the taps and swept back the shower curtain with a snap, anticipating warm clothes and a crackling fire in the stone fireplace. She felt like a mummy as she wrapped herself in one of the oversize bath towels from the linen closet. Toweling the damp ends of her hair, she walked into the bedroom and tossed her suitcase onto the bed.

"I hope there's another towel, or that you'll at least share yours," came a deep, unmistakable voice from the open bedroom door behind her.

She whirled around to face the intruder, wondering if she'd hit her head during her fall and was now hallucinating. A rather damp Nathan couldn't be leaning negligently against the door jamb as she clutched the top of her towel to her breast bone. She closed her eyes and opened them again. He was still there, dressed in jeans and a plaid shirt. His hair was plastered to the top of his head and spots of water darkened the shoulders of his shirt.

"Ah, I see I should have stayed quiet a little longer," he said, flashing a grin that matched the evil twinkle in his gray eyes. "It isn't often our revered water nymph allows a lowly mortal a glimpse of her, er . . . natural attributes."

"How in the blazes did you get in here?" she demanded, irritation with his suggestive tone helping her find her voice. His flowery words brought back images of tropical nights and laughing, uncomplicated days on the beach.

"Through the front door you left open," he explained,

not taking his eyes from her terry cloth encased figure. Her body began tingling with awareness as his heated gaze slowly traveled from the flushed skin at the top of her towel to her squirming feet. Then he began the process in reverse.

"Then you can easily find your way out again," she ordered through clenched teeth as she threw open her suitcase. Why did these things keep happening to her? Ever since she'd met Nathan Hartford her life had become a nightmare of mishaps.

"Now, Joanna, that's hardly neighborly." The words were barely out of his mouth before a terry cloth slipper went sailing past his ear. "I think it's time for a hasty retreat, old man," he muttered under his breath. The mate of the first absurd missile bounced harmlessly off the door he quickly shut behind him.

"Damn, I hope Brian was right. I certainly got a reaction from Joanna this time," Nathan said as he stared at the bedroom door, reaching up to stroke his mustache. What now?

His big plan wasn't much of a success, and he'd only been here ten minutes. He hadn't gotten Joanna's message until late last night, thanks to a temporary secretary's lack of organization. By the time he called Trent-Barringer this morning, Joanna was out of the office, so he asked if Diane was available. It seemed like such a good idea to follow Joanna down here. Why not?

"Because right now she can't stand the sight of you," he concluded, then bent to pick up the slipper that landed in the middle of the living room. Joanna had a good arm. Well, he wasn't going to leave, so he might as well do something useful. As he looked around the room the neat stack of logs in the fireplace, just waiting for a match, determined his next move.

The blaze was beginning to take hold when Nathan saw

the bedroom door begin to open out of the corner of his eye. He didn't move from his kneeling position, waiting with every muscle in his body tensed to see what Joanna would do when she discovered he was still here.

She walked cautiously into the room, carrying one slipper in her hand while she looked from side to side. Her hair hung loose around her shoulders, and much to his regret, she was covered from her neck to her ankles by a loose fitting, gauzy blouse and jeans. As she moved closer, he realized that she was looking for her other slipper.

"Looking for this," he asked quietly, holding up the slipper he'd found.

She jumped at the sound of his voice, apparently not having seen him with a chair and a lamp between them. "Thank you," she said tersely, moving to his side and snatching the slipper from his hand. Stalking over to the nearest armchair, she sat down to shove the slippers on her feet. For a minute she sat staring at him. "What are you doing here?"

"I talked to Diane when I missed you at the office, and thought a weekend retreat sounded like a great idea," he explained slowly, not wanting to make the wrong move or say the wrong thing. "A friend has a place not far from here, about a mile or so down the road. I thought I'd come over and see if we could work out some problems with our entertainment schedule while we were both here."

"Hmmmph," was her only answer.

Maybe she thought his story was as lame as he did, he decided, but he didn't think she'd like the real answer. He'd been furious when he'd gotten her message and been determined to confront her. Once he talked to Diane, he knew the trip was a legitimate reason for Joanna to back out of the picnic. However, it didn't have to mean they wouldn't spend time together this weekend. He'd lain awake last night anticipating it.

"I see you're not satisfied." He got to his feet and dusted off his hands, letting out a sigh of exasperation. "I'm sorry I barged in like that, but I found the front door wide open. No one answered when I called out, so I thought I would investigate." He gave a helpless shrug and finished with, "You know the rest."

"I fell in the mud," she managed in a whisper, ducking her head to stare at her feet.

"You fell in the mud?" He stood perfectly still for a moment as the words sank into his brain. Before he could help himself, he burst into laughter at the absurd picture that formed in his mind. As her face began to close up, he tried to contain his amusement, but thought of the usually poised and elegant Joanna plastered with mud was too much for his frayed nerves. He needed the release.

For a moment Joanna wanted to slap him. How dare he laugh at her? She bit back an angry rejoiner as she thought about how she must have looked, still a little indignant that she'd been so clumsy. Nathan's laughter was infectious, and she found herself giggling weakly at first, then wholeheartedly joining his deep timbred laughter. They both tried to contain their amusement, but each time they caught each other's eye, they would start all over again.

Finally she managed to regain some control, wiping away tears with one hand and holding her side with the other. She hadn't laughed enough lately, and it felt good. "I'm sorry about the slippers."

"You would have been sorrier if you'd hit me," he warned, his barely suppressed amusement taking the bite out of his words. "Though I don't think those things would have done a lot of damage. What do they weigh, about two or three ounces?"

"Wait until someone catches you in a towel and see

how you react." She sat up straighter, trying to look dignified as she clenched her toes inside her vicious weapons.

"Sounds like an interesting prospect," he mused as he
pretended to consider the situation. "Do you have any
candidates in mind?"

"Naturally *you* would feel that way. Men!"

"I think we'd better change the subject before I get into
trouble again. Can we call a truce for the evening?" He
waited for a minute, seeming to want her approval. "I
have some baking potatoes and the makings for a Caesar
salad for my half of our dinner. What have you got?"

She hesitated a minute. How could she refuse such a
reasonable offer? Though she'd anticipated a quiet weekend by herself, maybe this would be for the best. Why
not go ahead with the plan to get better acquainted? It still
sounded so silly, getting acquainted with the father of her
child.

"Bert said the refrigerator was stocked, and I'll bet
Celia put in some steaks. Why don't you take my car to
collect the rest of our dinner and get some dry clothes?
I'll get settled in while you're gone."

"Sounds like we're all set, doesn't it?" He didn't
move, almost as if he was waiting for her to change her
mind. When Joanna sat staring up at him he finally spoke.
"I'll walk back to my place. I'm already wet, so a little
more water won't hurt me. But I'll drive back. I don't
want to get caught in a downpour twice in one day."

He was gone without another word, as if he wanted to
escape before Joanna could change her mind. She sat staring into the fire, her hands folded protectively over her
stomach as she wondered if she'd done the right thing.

Hours later Joanna looked across the paper strewn table
at Nathan's dark head bent in concentration. She wondered
why she was tense. Although he'd continued to tease her

about her fall, his behavior had been impeccable all evening. They'd discussed only general topics over dinner before settling down to work. She also couldn't understand why she was disappointed. This was exactly what she wanted. The drive down must have exhausted her brain.

Her troubled thoughts ended abruptly as a clap of thunder ripped across the sky, setting off a wave of vibrations around the room. She noticed Nathan's hand clench around the pencil he was holding. He thrust back his chair and shot to his feet. As she watched, he stalked to the jacket he'd discarded earlier and searched through the pockets. When he found the missing object, he threw down the garment and walked to the fireplace. He began pacing, lighting one of the cigarettes he'd taken from his jacket.

"Is something wrong?"

"What?" he asked absently, taking a long drag on his cigarette, exhaling almost immediately. He stopped his pacing, almost bracing himself as the rumbling overhead started once more.

"I said, is something wrong? I've never seen you smoke."

He didn't answer as he began pacing again. He thrust his free hand through his hair, stopping at the base of his neck to knead his nape. Only the intermittent crashing sounds from above halted his movements. Joanna didn't understand what was happening. After a relaxing evening, there was a sudden sense of tension in the room.

"Nathan?" she asked softly as she approached him. Her voice made no impression on him, but she was determined to discover the reason behind his strange behavior. He jumped at the first touch of her hand, as if he'd forgotten her presence. Turning his head, he focused on her face.

"Are you feeling all right?"

He didn't answer immediately as he took in his surroundings. Then he shook off her hand, tossing his cigarette into the fire, and dropping onto the ottoman at his feet. "I'm sorry if I upset you. I have a migraine that's come and gone over the last few days," he explained, rubbing his hands over his face. "That racket outside seems to have set it off again. I've always hated thunderstorms. When I was a kid, I would almost suffocate under my pillow to block out the sound."

"You certainly picked a great place to live then," she said, attempting to mask her concern with humor. "St. Louis is going to be one continuous thunderbolt for the next few months. Wait until the height of the season. You'll think someone is setting off depth charges in your back yard."

"Thank you, Pollyanna. Is that anything to tell a suffering man?" His laugh was weak as he pressed his thumb and forefinger to the bridge of his nose, closing his eyes as if to shut out the pain.

Joanna watched helplessly, wanting to ease his pain but unsure what to do. After a moment's consideration she walked purposely to the chair behind him, pushed it forward, and sat down.

"Hey, what's going on?" Nathan gasped as she pulled him back between her knees.

"Just hold still and tilt your head back," she ordered. "I used to do this for Dad when he'd get tensed up, so we'll try it on a migraine. Close your eyes and relax."

As soon as he was comfortable, her fingers began working over his neck and shoulders. In a few minutes she could feel the muscles unknotting under her massaging fingers. Then she moved her hands upward to the taut skin under his ears, repeating the same treatment. From there she worked lightly over his temples. She worked in silence with an occasional murmur of approval from her patient. Soon he grew quiet and his breathing deepened.

Joanna watched her fingers continue to work with a detachment. Nathan looked as vulnerable as a child with his eyes closed, the lines of his face relaxed. Fleetingly she remembered his tender smile while playing with little Jeffrey. Letting out an involuntary sigh she recalled the first time she'd seen him smile in Nassau.

Jerking her head up she realized what she'd been about to do. Her lips had been a mere inch from his forehead, which was now cleared of furrows of pain. She tried to dismiss the traitorous action as her hands moved automatically over his skin.

She couldn't be falling in love with this impossible man. Yes, there was a physical attraction, compounded by the romantic surroundings of their first meeting. Their confrontations over the past few weeks were the result of sexual antagonism, nothing more. However, the memory of their night together at her apartment mocked her rationalization.

What a fool she was. She hadn't been fighting against Nathan, she'd been fighting her own latent feelings. Loving someone always meant pain and loss. Her parents and Albert Trent left her through death, and Keith through betraying her trust. A sob lodged in her throat. Nathan wasn't a permanent fixture in her life either. Was that why she couldn't make a decision about telling him about the baby? She couldn't face the inevitable pain and anguish?

She lifted her hands abruptly, standing up slowly to allow Nathan to lean back against the chair cushion before she walked to the fireplace. It was safer away from the temptation of his drowsy body. She rested her head against the mantel, shutting her eyes against the bright flames. She tried to empty her mind of all thoughts with little success.

"Jo? What's the matter?" Nathan's concerned voice came from directly behind her. His hands came up to rest lightly on her shoulders, burning through the thin material of her blouse.

"Nothing." She was amazed that her voice sounded so normal. "I thought you were asleep, so I stopped."

"It certainly had the desired effect. Thank you." His voice was still concerned as he unwittingly continued to torture her. "Are you sure you're all right? Your muscles feel like they're tied in knots. Shall I return the favor?"

"I'm just tired from the drive down. I'll take a dip in the whirlpool before I go to bed tonight," she lied quickly, her mind only half functioning. Her newly discovered feelings, coupled with his presence, were stretching her nerves unbearably. The inner tension was almost painful as his hands began to gently knead the muscles at the base of her neck.

"Really, Nathan, there's absolutely no need for this." She turned, hoping to avoid further physical contact. However, he didn't step back as she anticipated. She found her nose buried in the soft material of his shirt. Her balance was thrown off as she stumbled to avoid falling back into the fireplace. Clutching at his shoulders, she allowed her head to rest against his chest for one weak moment. It was a melancholy luxury to be held against him. His spicy aftershave and traces of tobacco blended with his natural scent, filling her senses. Abruptly the spell was broken as his hands tightened at her waist.

"Joanna?" His husky voice fluttered down her spine, causing her to catch her breath as she met his worried gaze. His expression was soft and tender. She wished time would stand still so she could savor the warmth in his gray eyes forever.

She accepted the tentative touch of his lips as a natural extension of his concern. Her raw emotions received the balm of his tenderness gladly. The last, disturbing half hour was lost in the oblivion of his sweet embrace. All the love that she'd repressed seemed to flow through her as she awakened to his touch.

When Nathan's arms tightened, pulling her firmly against his hard body, she responded without hesitation. Her hands tangling in his thick hair, showing her approval with small sounds deep in her throat as he deepened the kiss. She parted her lips willingly to allow him more freedom, glorying in the ability to demonstrate her chaotic emotions.

Together they sank to the soft carpeting before the fire. Joanna welcomed the weight of Nathan's body. Her tongue twined with his playfully and he answered her caress with a gravelly moan of approval. She wasn't aware of anything, but the man holding her. His strong hands moved over the soft material of her sweater, and the lacy underwear beneath, removing the garments from her heated skin. In turn, she moved her hands under the pliant material of his chamois shirt to knead the taut muscles of his back.

This wasn't enough. Her fingers loosened the buttons of his shirt to explore the broad expanse beneath. Abruptly Nathan raised his head from where his lips teased the upper swell of her breasts. "Slowly, my sweet nymph," he whispered hoarsely as his lips wandered over her flushed face. "I want this to be very special."

"Nathan, please?" She grasped his head in an attempt to bring his lips back to her own.

"Do you know how beautiful you are, love? Your hair spread out around you, the shadows of the flames playing over your sleek body?" His lips moved against hers with each syllable as his warm, callused hand circled the fullness of her breast. "I want to spend the rest of the weekend here in your arms."

Joanna murmured her assent as he increased the pressure of his mouth. As his hands moved to caress her waist she arched in anticipation. The tantalizing contact of his hands instilled a need for a physical bond. She urged his firm chest against her swollen breasts. Her restless fingers explored the hollow of his lower back, delving beneath the waistband of his trousers.

"Easy, love, we have all the time in the world," he said softly, trailing his lips over her neck to the rapid pulse at the base. His mouth left a moist trail as he followed the path made by his hands. Finally he came to rest, brushing the soft bristles of his mustache against Joanna's hip bone.

She closed her eyes, savoring the electric rush that coursed through her body. Her newly discovered love only sweetened the glorious feelings he engendered. She floated in a magical realm of sensations as Nathan gently parted her legs to allow him access to the soft skin of her inner thigh. Her body tensed for a moment as his ardent mouth followed his hands. She relaxed under his tender ministrations only to tense against his wandering lips and moist tongue. She arched upward to accept his tribute to her femininity.

She gripped his shoulders as the inner convulsions began, spreading through her body. Gradually the palpitations ceased, she had no time to relax in the glowing aftermath. Nathan moved swiftly, removing his clothing as he kissed his way back up her body. She was engulfed once more in a haze of passion as he entered her slowly.

She welcomed the gift of his desire. They moved together, blending their individual need into a single quest for fulfillment. Nathan moved to his side, allowing her more freedom to express her passion. He controlled the thrust of her movements, lightly cupping the pliant globes of her buttocks. Leisurely he led them upward to the plane of release.

Joanna cried out his name as the vibration of completion began once more. She cradled Nathan in her arms as he trembled in release. They remained motionless in a close embrace, sharing the languid aftermath of their lovemaking. Finally she roused herself to gently kiss the heated flesh of Nathan's chest.

"Joanna?"

"Mmmmmm," she murmured as she watched her index finger forge a trail through the dark hair that covered his chest. She really didn't want to talk, but bask in the languid feeling of her body, the warmth of Nathan's skin and the protective shelter of his arms.

"I've have an idea about the rest of the weekend," he went on, his words a deep rumble under her ear. As his hand stroked up and down her arm, she really wasn't paying attention to his words.

"Whatever."

Suddenly she was on her back with Nathan looming over her, his hands planted on either side of her head. When she tried to link her fingers around his neck, he jerked his head to the side. But there was a smile on his lips. "This is important. Will you pay attention for at least a minute or two?"

She gave him a secretive smile, trailing her finger from his chin to the middle of his chest. "Only if you make it worth my while."

"That's a promise," he returned, his eyes intent as if promising more than a passionate night in his arms. "Now, are you going to pay attention?"

She nodded solemnly, but began to feel uneasy about what he would say. What she was doing was dangerous, escaping from reality to indulge in a fantasy that couldn't last. That was what started her problems in Nassau, forgetting about the outside world and recklessly enjoying the moment. But she wanted this time with Nathan. This would be a magic memory that she could carry with her, no matter what happened in the future.

"This weekend we're going to forget about Trent-Barringer and Hartford Consolidated. You and I are going to exist in a vacuum, our own little universe." He paused as if waiting for her to interrupt, or refuse to consider the idea. When Joanna lay still beneath him, his expression became less guarded and his body began to relax against hers. "On Monday we might have the same problems and the same disagreements, but until then, we put everything on hold. Agreed?"

"I think that's a wonderful plan," she replied and framed his face between her hands, pulling his head down until his lips were a fraction of an inch from her own. She'd planned to think about her future this weekend, but putting it off a few more days wouldn't matter that much, would it? Her friends wanted her to spend more time with Nathan, and this was an ideal opportunity.

"You haven't gone to sleep, have you?" he murmured, his mustache tickling her upper lip with each word.

"No, I was just wondering what you'd like to do next. Got any ideas?" she asked provocatively, looking deep into the gray eyes that held a mixture of amusement, hesitation, and invitation. All her anxiety and pessimism of the previous weeks faded miraculously under his warm regard. She had nothing to lose, and everything to gain by taking a chance this time.

"I have quite a few ideas, though it might take more than a weekend to explore the possibilities."

She gave her approval with actions instead of words, moving her head slightly to bring their lips together. Twining her arms around Nathan's neck, she welcomed his weight as he settled against her. Neither of them noticed or cared whether the storm outside continued, they were more pleasantly occupied for the rest of the night.

EIGHT

Nathan whistled happily as he foraged through the refrigerator to prepare breakfast. The morning called for something special, though he wasn't sure his culinary skills were up to it, he was going to try. As he collected bacon, margarine, and eggs, he still couldn't believe that he was here with Joanna. Even the weather was cooperating; last night's storm was only a memory as sunshine streamed into the bay window of the breakfast room.

Placing the bacon into a heating pan on the stove he thought of how tempting Joanna looked a half hour ago when he woke up. The vulnerable appeal of her sleeping face filled him with tenderness, so he'd let her sleep. Full of excess energy, he went for a morning run and had been inspired with the idea of serving her breakfast in bed. Men did crazy things when they were in love. And he was a man in love. The revelation came to him as he sat on the edge of the bed this morning watching Joanna. Nothing could be more beautiful.

Now he knew why she'd been such an obsession since the moment they'd met in Nassau. He'd finally found the woman he was going to spend the rest of his life with. Apparently he'd been searching for her without realizing it for the past few years. She added the missing piece to his life, bringing him a new sense of contentment. That was why he had lost his usual poise and self-control whenever she was around.

The hiss of the bacon beginning to fry brought him out of his romantic daze. He needed to keep his mind on the matter at hand, unless he wanted breakfast to be a burnt offering. In spite of his euphoria at his discovery, he knew that there was still some rough ground to cover. Joanna didn't want to trust him, though her acquiesence last night was a promising sign.

He would use the weekend to begin building a foundation for their future. She was still a little skittish, but he was making progress. All he had to do was be patient. Then he laughed out loud at his own foolishness. His impatience was what was continually getting him in trouble with the lady. Knowing that he loved her wasn't going to suddenly curb his persistent nature.

"What's so funny?" asked a sleepy voice from the doorway of the kitchen.

"Nothing, I hope. Unless I manage to burn our breakfast," he replied, leaning back against the counter to give her an appreciative smile. Now he knew he had it bad. Her hair was tousled around her shoulders, her eyes still puffy from sleep, but she looked gorgeous in her white satin robe.

"Are you a morning person? You should have warned me." Though her words were teasing, she gave him a wary look, as if she wasn't quite sure how to handle the situation. "I don't think I would have let you stay if I'd known."

"How about some coffee, would that help?" He wanted to catch her in his arms and kiss away her doubts, but he was a little uneasy that she might not be joking. There was still a lot he had to learn about the lady, so he'd go easy, for now.

"No, I can't," she answered abruptly, and gave a philosophical shrug. "I'm cutting back on caffeine these days."

"How about some juice instead? Think that will help?" he asked and turned toward the refrigerator.

"We'll see," she murmured, finally moving away from the doorway as she spoke.

Nathan pulled out the orange juice container and poured her a glass, moving slowly. He tried not to smile over the absurd situation. They were both acting like polite strangers, afraid to do or say the wrong thing. "Well, a little vitamin C never hurt anybody." He turned to hand her the glass, but stopped with the glass halfway between them. She was staring over his shoulder with a look of horrified fascination, one hand over her mouth and the other spread over her stomach. "Joanna, what's the matter?"

"Nothing, nothing, really," she barely managed as she backed away from him. Her eyes never waivered, her expression making him look at the stove to see if something had caught fire. "I'll pass on breakfast. Got to get dressed."

She bolted out of the room before he could say a word, her hand still clamped over her mouth. Nathan stared after her, but a pop of bacon fat from the pan made him turn back to the stove. He turned off the burner with a quick twist of the dial and moved the pan to another burner. Once he was sure everything was secure, he turned to head for the bedroom.

Was she coming down with something? He knew she'd had the flu recently. What else could it be? *Just yesterday she was craving bacon, then ran out of the room before she took a bite*. Brian's words flashed into his mind, bringing him up short before he stepped out of the kitchen. He felt hot and cold in a brief instant, wanting both to run into the bedroom and stay where he was. Was it such a crazy idea? Was Joanna pregnant?

Nathan sat down at the breakfast table, unaware of what he was doing. He didn't want to believe it. Surely she would have told him. Or would she? She hadn't expected to see him again after she left Nassau, and had been in shock the night he'd walked back into her life. That was the only way to describe her reaction. Until today, he'd never given it a second thought, merely thinking she'd been surprised.

So, what did he do now? Did he confront her, or wait to see if she would tell him? He could be imagining the whole thing, because of a silly coincidence and Brian's chance comment about his wife. Maybe it was wishful thinking on his part. Beneath the numb feeling there was a glimmer of hope. This was something that would tie Joanna to him.

Jumping to his feet, he paced around the room. What did he do? Was he damned if he said something, or damned if he didn't? His first priority was getting Joanna to trust him again, and that didn't mean grilling her about her health. One look at the cooling bacon made up his mind, and he dumped the contents of the pan into the trash. He would wait.

This weekend was supposed to be an escape from reality. However, he couldn't get the picture of Joanna carrying his baby out of his mind. No, he wouldn't question her, not until he was sure of what he was doing. What else could he do?

"Here we are, enough wood to keep us going for the rest of the night. Bert deserves a sizeable tip for keeping it dry on the porch."

Joanna jumped at the sound of his overly cheerful voice,

and hated herself for it. She'd been acting like this all day, trying to decide what to do. Every time Nathan gave her a few minutes alone, she replayed this morning's near disaster in her mind. He hadn't given the slightest hint that he suspected anything, but all she could think about was Brian's comments at lunch about Chris.

If he suspected he would have said something by now, wouldn't he? As she watched him add another log to the fire, she wondered for the hundredth time if she should tell him tonight. She'd been tempted so many times today, while they were walking through the woods, when they'd taken one of Bert's boats out on the lake and again at dinner. But each time she'd found another excuse to delay. If she was this indecisive at work, she'd be bankrupt by now, she thought in disgust at her weakness. But she just couldn't bring herself to form the words.

"Does the fire meet with madam's approval?"

Joanna blinked and focused on Nathan's still figure by the fire. She hadn't seen him move while lost in her internal debate. His face was solemn despite his teasing question.

"It's absolutely incredible," she answered, shaking off her troubled thoughts. The day had been perfect, and she wasn't going to waste any more of it worrying. There was plenty of time to tell Nathan next week.

"Flattery will get you anything you want," he stated as he came to join her on the couch. He settled close to her, draping his arm around her shoulder.

She snuggled against his side, laying her head on his shoulder. During moments like this she was sure he didn't know. He'd seemed anxious to touch her whenever it was possible. If they were walking, he'd hold her hand. When they stopped to watch a bird or a rabbit, he held her close to her side. It brought back memories of their days in the tropics, but the sense of urgency of those days was gone.

In its place was a sense of warmth and security. Something she wanted to cherish, if only for today.

She closed her eyes, savoring the moment. The shrill ringing of the phone abruptly brought her out of her daydreams.

"Want me to get that, sleepy head?" Nathan was looking down at her with an indulgent smile. Glancing at the clock on the mantel, she realized that she must have fallen asleep.

"No, I'm closer," she murmured unable to suppress a yawn. Moving slowly, she reached over the arm of the couch to pick up the receiver. At first the voice at the other end of the phone didn't register. Then Joanna strove to clear her drowsy mind.

"Diane, is that you? Wait a minute, slow down. I can't understand you."

Her entire body went rigid as she continued to listen, unaware she was opening and closing her hand repeatedly, as if to punctuate each word. She wasn't aware of Nathan moving to her side until he pried her fingers away from the receiver.

"Diane? This is Nathan, what's going on?" he barked into the phone. "You've just put Joanna into shock."

"George has been taken to the hospital. His car ran off the road and hit a telephone pole," Diane managed weakly. "He's been unconscious since they brought him in." She broke off in a sobbing breath.

"Okay, take it easy," he instructed gently. "Was there any internal damage?"

"The doctor said a broken leg and a head wound," she managed unevenly.

"All right, now listen to this closely," he told her firmly. "As soon as I hang up, call my uncle, he and Helen can wait at the hospital with you. Where are you?

County Hospital, good. We'll leave as soon as Joanna is fit to travel, so take care until we get there."

"Joanna?" Nathan spoke her name softly as he hung up the phone. She was staring at the fire, but he was sure she didn't see anything in front of her. He called her name again, and placed his hand on her shoulder. It was enough to rouse her. She looked up at him, her face pale, her eyes beginning to fill with tears. He reacted immediately, his arms pulling her to her feet and into a comforting embrace as a tight band began to constrict around his heart.

Almost the instant her head touched his shoulder, she dissolved into uncontrollable tears. Nathan held her patiently, allowing her the release she needed as he felt his own world crumbling around him. Apparently there was more to her relationship with Collins than anyone suspected, or perhaps she hadn't suspected it herself until this moment.

When she didn't seem able to stop crying, Nathan knew he had to do something. He held her away from him, giving her a slight shake to capture her attention. "Joanna, we need to leave."

She stood staring at him for a minute as though she couldn't understand what he wanted. When he gave her another shake, she took a deep breath and wiped at her cheeks with the back of her hand.

"Are you all right?" he asked roughly, his own emotions were precarious as he searched her tear stained face.

"I'm sorry I fell apart like that," she managed between ragged breaths, still trying to control her tears. "My parents were killed in a car accident when I was very young, and I guess it brought back those memories. I just can't believe this is happening."

"Go get your things together while I put out the fire," he instructed, purposely keeping his tone brisk. She needed to keep busy, not let her imagination frighten her. "Now get a move on, we have a long drive ahead of us."

"Us? What about my car?"

"I'll call Bert Tracy and see what he can do. Right now, you concentrate on getting back to the city. How long will it take you to pack?"

Joanna didn't answer immediately. Her face betrayed her wandering thoughts. Nathan knew she was on the verge of another bout of tears.

"Joanna, don't you dare start crying," he snapped. He didn't want to play the heavy, but he wasn't sure he could stand to see her crying again over another man. When she didn't move, he clamped his hands on her shoulders and marched her toward the bedroom. "Now get your stuff together. You have fifteen minutes."

After one bewildered look, she reacted just as he anticipated. No one liked to be treated like a child, even during a crisis. Shaking off his hands, she said with stiff dignity, "There is no need to shove me around. I'll be ready in my own good time."

"You're losing time by arguing. You now have fourteen minutes to go," he stated, hoping to fuel her anger. Her temper would get her through the rough ground of preparing to leave.

"I'm not a child," she snapped before turning abruptly and stalking into the bedroom.

Joanna was ready to leave in ten minutes while Nathan called Bert to ask him to close up the cabin and made arrangements for Joanna's car. He didn't say a word when she came out of the bedroom, but hustled her into his car. After a stop at his friend's cabin, they were ready to leave. When he settled himself in the car Joanna was sitting on the edge of her seat, her hands tightly clenched in her lap.

"Here take this," he ordered, holding out a thermos cup and a yellow pill.

"What is it?"

"It's a harmless motion sickness tablet. It might help you get some sleep on the drive back to St. Louis," he replied evenly.

"No, thank you," she managed to whisper and settled down in the seat, crossing her arms over her chest.

He wanted to protest, but changed his mind as he glanced at her profile. Her eyelids were already beginning to close. She had been sleeping before Diane's frantic call, and the last emotional half hour had taken its toll. By the time they reached the highway ten minutes later, she'd dropped off to sleep.

Nathan wished he could block out his pain so easily as he stared down the dark highway.

"Joanna." Her name was being called from a long distance. "Hey, Joanna, come on. You're making a nasty habit of falling asleep in my car."

She opened her eyes slowly, trying to focus on the face that was a few inches from hers.

"I thought that might bring you around," Nathan said with a slight chuckle. "Don't talk, drink this first." He thrust a Styrofoam cup in her hand, half filled with hot tea.

"Where are we?" she asked after the first gulp of hot liquid, her mind beginning to function again.

"At an all night donut shop a couple of blocks from the hospital."

"We couldn't possibly be in Clayton already," she exclaimed in astonishment.

"There wasn't a lot of traffic," he murmured, making her wonder how fast he had driven while she slept.

"Why didn't you go straight to the hospital?" she demanded as she drained her cup and looked out at the deserted, dimly lit parking lot for the first time.

"I thought you might need a little reviving to face the real world."

"Thank you," she responded with a weak smile as the full impact of his words crossed her alert mind. The memory of the night she watched the policemen talking in quiet whispers to the whimpering babysitter as Joanna stood peering through the banister was clear in her mind. "Nathan, I'm frightened."

"Don't worry," he reassured her, laying his hand over hers that were tightly clasped in her lap. "I called the hospital when we arrived. There hasn't been any change, but there's no need for concern. It takes time for the body to recover from a shock like George had. Now, how do you feel?"

"Fine, just a little groggy. Nothing that a little more tea won't cure," she assured him. "After that, can we please go to the hospital?"

"Sure, honey, right now," he answered with a grim smile. With her hair tousled from sleep and the pleading note in her voice, she looked and sounded about ten years old. He wanted to hold her again, but knew he would be torturing himself. The strained look on her face clearly showed that her thoughts were centered on George Collins.

As they approached the nurse's station twenty minutes later, Joanna reached over to grasp Nathan's hand. His reassuring squeeze gave her the support she had sought blindly. She returned the pressure, and stepped forward to ask, "Excuse me, can you tell me where I can find Dr. Dreyer?"

"Are you Ms. Trent? He had an emergency about fifteen minutes ago, but he left word he'd meet you in the waiting room as soon as he could," the diminutive woman answered gently, a comforting smile on her gamine face. "Mr. Collins is resting comfortably."

No one spoke as they stood at the entrance of the waiting room. Diane sat red-eyed at one end of the vinyl couch, one hand absently pulling apart a tissue, and Helen sat beside her holding her other hand, while Evan stood across the room looking out the window. He turned when Nathan spoke his name.

"Have you heard anything from the doctor?" he asked his nephew, noting Joanna's drawn face.

"Nothing else. The nurse said he'll be up when he's through with another patient," Nathan replied as he released Joanna's hand. His aunt came to stand beside them and placed a comforting arm around Joanna's waist.

"Really, Helen, I'm fine," Joanna protested, but allowed the other woman to lead her to the couch. "I slept most of the way back."

Helen ignored her reassurances, insisting that she should sit down. Joanna didn't resist, and one look at Diane's tortured face made her forget her own worries.

"Take it easy, hon," Joanna whispered when Helen moved to talk to her husband and nephew, who were holding a quiet conversation by the window. "It's going to be all right. The doctor isn't worried, and he's taken care of George most of his life. Okay?"

"Yes, of course," Diane managed through a drawn out sniff. She sat up straight, taking deep breaths to remain calm. "I just haven't gotten over the shock of the phone call yet. Dr. Dreyer's nurse tried to contact you right away, then the answering service. I barely got back from the Cape, in fact I almost didn't come back tonight. You wouldn't have known anything until Sunday night."

"But you did come back," Joanna assured her, placing her hand over Diane's agitated fingers that were destroying another tissue. "And I'm here now. That's all that's important. Just—" she broke off as a tall, swarthy man appeared in the doorway. She rose and hurried across the room.

"Joanna, my dear, don't look so alarmed," Dr. Dreyer said gruffly. He'd known the Trent and Collins families since the time she came down with the measles soon after being adopted. His blue eyes narrowed as he studied her pale face. "George is fine. His leg is fractured in two places, and it's been set. He's in good shape with a few other cuts and bruises. Since he has a mild concussion, we're going to keep him a few days as a precaution. So take that look off your face, I don't need another patient tonight."

She attempted to smile, but gave up the effort. "I haven't called Aunt Tess yet. I thought I'd wait until morning, if you think that's all right."

"I took care of that myself, since you were out of town," he informed her, "just as soon as we knew his condition. Your mother will call you in the morning for more details, and you have some fast talking to do. When she asked where you were, I explained that you were traveling back from the lake with a young man.

"Now, young lady, that should give you something besides George to worry about until tomorrow. From what Dr. Jessup tells me you have your own health to think about right now as well."

"Some friend you are." She chuckled slightly, then she jerked her head toward the group near the window. "You didn't say anything to Mother about the—"

"No, I haven't said a word," he returned, his gaze following her to the tall, dark haired man by the window. "However, this isn't something you put off for much longer. Have you told the father yet?"

"No, the timing hasn't been right," she mumbled, feeling like a child being chastised. There was something about the authoritative pose of doctors.

"I can't say I like it much, but I'll keep mum as long you take care of yourself," he conceded, his frown deepening. "Now I'm going to check on that idiot brother of yours. If I thought it would do any good, I'd have him give you a lecture."

"Fat chance," she returned, sharing a conspiratal smile with her old friend. Both of them knew her brother was the last person to give her a talk on sensible behavior.

"Humph," was the doctor's only reply before he stomped out of the room.

"Anything new?" asked a voice behind her. She twisted around, and to her relief, discovered Evan behind her, not Nathan.

"He's going to check on George now. Everything seems to be fine," she explained. Giving him a bright smile, she wondered how much of the conversation he'd overheard and understood. "I think I'll stay a little longer, but the rest of you should go home and get some sleep."

"That's probably for the best. I'll make sure Joanna gets home," Nathan put in from behind her. When she turned, she was startled by the grim set of his expression. His dark eyes were trained on his uncle. "I'll walk you down to the car."

"That isn't necessary, dear," his aunt assured him.

"I need a cigarette right now," he muttered, looking at Evan for some support. Nathan still didn't look at Joanna as the older man shepherded Diane and Helen out of the room.

"I thought you quit smoking," came Helen's voice from the hallway as Joanna began pacing the empty room. Nathan's reply was quick and short, "I did."

As she walked the length of the room, Joanna realized how selfish she'd been taking Nathan's support for granted. He had barely said a word since they arrived at the hospital. Everything else had gone out of her head after hearing about George's accident. Although Nathan didn't know of her true relationship to George, he'd gone

to great length to help her. When he returned she owed
him a long overdo explanation about George. There were
too many other misunderstandings between them, and this
one should be easy to handle.

However, there wasn't time. He barely walked in the
room when Dr. Dreyer returned. At the broad smile on
the doctor's face she ran across the room, Nathan only a
step behind her. Unconsciously she reached for his hand
as she waited for the doctor to speak.

"You two can get some sleep now. He came around a
few minutes ago and is now sleeping like a baby. He told
me that Joanna's not to worry, he's still with us."

She wanted to shout for joy as her worry dropped away.
Mindful of where she was, Joanna did the first thing that
came to mind. She flung her arms around Nathan's neck,
laughing almost uncontrollably. His arms closed around
her back for a moment in a crushing hug before he moved
his hands to her shoulders.

"Now that you have that out of your system, I'm taking
you home," he ordered in a husky voice.

"Excellent idea, young man, and I don't want to see
either of you before noon tomorrow, understand?"

The sky was beginning to lighten as Nathan parked in
front of Joanna's apartment. Neither of them had spoken
during the drive from the hospital.

"What time is it?" she asked as they walked up the
stairs.

"I'm not sure," he murmured, running a weary hand
through his hair as she fumbled with the lock.

"Nathan, you're almost dead on your feet," she
exclaimed as she opened the door. He was leaning heavily
against the wall, almost as if he planned to stay there
indefinitely. Tension lines creased his forehead, showing
the past few hours had taken their toll. His shoulders were
bowed and the erect hold of his head looked painful,

reminding her of his headache the previous night. "I can't let you drive around in this condition."

"What do you suggest?" he asked flatly without moving.

"Only the spare room. I'm responsible for the state you're in, and I couldn't hold up if there was another accident."

"You're right, although I'd planned to sleep in the car," he explained, then broke off when a jaw popping yawn overcame him. "I couldn't see making a trip to the hotel only to turn around to come back in a few hours."

"Come back?"

"If you'd think about it for a minute, you'd figure it out." His tone was dry and his mouth quirked slightly to the side in a semblance of amusement. "We started out with two cars Friday, now there's just mine. Bert won't have yours back until sometime tonight. I'm your temporary chauffeur, unless you plan to walk to the hospital."

"Good, then you can go back down and fetch the luggage we forgot to bring up," she ordered, stung by his patronizing tone. "I'll see to your room."

She turned away, not caring if he stayed or went. Clearing off the bed in the guest room helped to work off her temporary pique. She was trying to remember the last time the bed had been slept in when the front door slammed. Walking toward the door, she knew she should apologize for her childish outburst, but Nathan didn't seem to be concerned about anyone's mood.

"I don't care if I have to sleep standing up," he muttered as he walked down the hallway, "that room better be ready for me." He tossed his suitcase on the bed at the end of his speech, then hoisted hers again.

"My room," she said quickly, trying not to flinch when he said under his breath something that sounded like *I remember*. She stood in the middle of the room unable to move. Everything had been take care of, including fresh towels, yet she still stood there. Nathan pulled up short just inside the door. His frown deepening as she inwardly struggled to come up with a rational explanation.

"I thought I'd see if . . ." she let the words drift away when her voice came out breathy and hesitant. Taking a deep swallow, she tried again. "Would you like something to eat or anything else before I go to bed?"

"Nothing." He brushed past her and made quick work of opening his suitcase. "Just tell me where I wash up."

"Across the hall." She gave an absent wave that could include anything outside the room before clearing her throat. "Well, if you're sure there's nothing," she managed as she edged slowly toward the door, still reluctant to leave. "I'd be glad to fix you a sandwich or something, dinner seems such a long time ago."

"Nothing," he repeated emphatically, unbuttoning his shirt, but never taking his eyes off her retreating figure.

Reluctantly she turned to leave, but still couldn't move. She hadn't thanked him for all the trouble he'd gone to on her behalf. Whirling around to make up for her thoughtlessness, she was surprised to discover he hadn't moved. He was watching her with a strange brooding expression, his hands poised over the platen of his shirt.

"Nathan, I—"

"Unless you plan to spend the night here, I suggest you make your exit immediately, because I'm getting undressed right now, with or without an audience." He dropped his hands to his belt with exaggerated care.

He didn't move for a moment when the door slammed behind her. For a few minutes he stared at the spot where Joanna had been, then he sat down heavily on the bed. His hands came up to cover his face, rubbing over the skin in slow movements. Brian was wrong. Joanna loved George very deeply. Her actions tonight made it all too clear. Although she could respond to him physically, all her love was given to another man.

He felt as if his heart had been ripped out and run over by a tank. Yesterday morning he'd been filled with a sense of anticipation at the possibility that Joanna might be pregnant. He'd been awed by the prospect of becoming a father. Now, he was numb. Even if Joanna were carrying his child, she was in love with another man.

Listlessly he dropped back on the bed, not caring he was still dressed. He stared up at the ceiling, wondering how his life had gotten so complicated. It had begun as a simple matter of looking up a business associate in Nassau. His eyelids seemed weighted down and he gave into the oblivion of sleep before he could think about what to do in the morning.

_____ NINE _____

Light was streaming in the windows when Joanna opened her eyes the next morning. She couldn't orient herself at first, or understand why she'd slept in her clothes. The memories of the previous night came rushing back in a flash of images; the final episode foremost in her mind. She'd made an absolute fool of herself.

She groaned and rolled over to stare at the ceiling. One thought ran over and over in her mind. She was hopelessly in love with Nathan, and didn't have a clue on how to straighten out the mess she'd managed to make of her life in a few short months. The rolling of her stomach was a poignant reminder of the most pressing issue.

As tears threatened, she threw the pillow she clutched to her chest onto the floor and grabbed for the soda crackers. Lying in bed wasn't going to solve anything, she decided fatalistically. She was able to get to her feet and head for the bathroom a few minutes later. A shower and fresh clothes would be a good start before she called her mother. After that she would simply have to play it by ear.

The apartment was silent as she carefully walked to the kitchen; the guest room door was closed. She punched out her mother's number automatically, keeping a watchful eye on the door to Nathan's room. It was ironic that he was sleeping in the room that she planned to convert into a nursery. How was she going to face him this morning?

"Mother, this is Joanna."

"Yes, dear. How is George coming along?"

"So far so good, according to Dr. Dreyer. George regained consciousness before I left the hospital, but I didn't see him. He was already asleep when I talked to the doctor, then Nathan and I were ordered to go home."

"Oh, yes, Nathan," Amanda Trent murmured with an amused tone. "Who exactly is he, or am I being too personal? I'm just maternal enough to want to know about the man who spent a weekend with my daughter."

"Dear Dr. Dreyer," Joanna muttered under her breath.

"What, dear?"

"I wasn't spending the weekend the way you think," she said quickly, hastily crossing her fingers as she realized she probably had. "I didn't know you had such a trashy mind. Aha, I heard that snicker. You almost had me convinced with that heavy parent routine."

"You know better. You're old enough to do as you choose, but I admit I'm curious."

"He's a client, and George's new boss. It was lucky for me he was at the lake this weekend," Joanna explained, sticking as close to the truth as possible. "I nearly went to pieces when Diane called. I don't think I could have made it home without him."

"You would have managed if you had to, dear. That strong will of yours helps in dealing with a crisis. However, I'm glad someone was with you, even if it was some handsome devil who devours you with his eyes every time he looks at you," her mother said as if reciting a piece of poetry.

"Where did you come up with such lurid nonsense?"

"George. You know he can be quite lyrical when he puts his mind to it," Amanda replied, laughing at the choking sounds coming from her daughter. "He called from Seattle, but said not to worry, because he'd made sure Nathan kept his distance."

"That devil," Joanna practically yelled into the receiver, forgetting the need for quiet. "Wait until I get my hands on my brother, that louse will have more than a broken—" Her threat was cut short by a noise behind her. Slowly turning her head she found Nathan standing a few feet away, dressed only in a short, dark blue terry cloth robe.

"I think George has enough bruises as it is. Joanna, are you there?"

"Yes, yes, I was distracted for a minute. I suppose you're right, about the bruises, I mean."

"Are you all right? You suddenly sound a little strange."

"Yes, I'm fine," she assured her mother before clamping her hand over the receiver and warned him in a whisper, "My mother, don't say anything."

"Joanna, who are you talking to? Or should I take a lucky guess?"

"No!" She couldn't believe this was happening. She was thirty years old and lying, badly, to her mother because a man was in her apartment. Dr. Dreyer was going to pay for his little joke. Or was this retribution for her weeks of evasion? "Look, I'll call you tonight at Aunt Tess's after I've seen George."

"Fine, dear, but you haven't escaped as easily as you think. My curiosity is definitely aroused."

"Just trust me," Joanna stated with more confidence than she felt. Amanda Trent would be amazed at what her daughter had to tell her. Whatever she was anticipating, it wasn't the news that she was going to be a grandmother.

"All right, dear, and, Joanna . . . say good morning to Nathan for me, will you?"

She hung up the phone with a grim smile and turned to the silent man. "My mother says good morning."

"I'll have to meet her sometime," he said, smiling at the face Joanna made, seeming to have thrown off the bad temper of a few hours earlier. "She must be quite a lady."

"Would you like some breakfast, or should I say brunch?" she asked briskly totally unprepared for his good humor. She opened the refrigerator to block out the disturbing sight of his enticing body.

"I could eat everything in the refrigerator. I'm ravenous."

"How about an omelette, toast, and coffee to start?" she asked with her head hidden behind the door. If he asked for bacon, she was in trouble.

"Great, I'll shave and get into some presentable clothes. Will that give you enough time?"

"Plenty, don't rush," she answered as she placed the ingredients on the counter. *Take all the time you need, and maybe I can find my brains in the next hour or so, especially if we continue all this civilized behavior.* "I'll mix everything and put it on the stove when you're ready."

"Give me fifteen minutes." He took a step toward the bathroom, then hesitated. "Joanna, about last night. I want to apologize." He held up his hand to forestall her protest. "No, don't say a word. I was tired and unreasonable when you were trying to be thoughtful. You'd been through enough without me venting my temper on you. Am I forgiven?"

"Yes, of course." She kept her eyes on the food in front of her, concentrating on lining up the eggs in a straight row. He couldn't see the tears forming in her eyes.

Damn her erratic hormones. Before he could say anything else, the phone rang.

"Hello? Yes, Helen, I'm fine. As a matter of fact, I only woke up a few minutes ago. Nathan? You say he didn't come back to the hotel last night? Really?"

She jumped at the shout of laughter from behind her. Covering the receiver, she made frantic motions for Nathan to disappear, which to her surprise, he did. His matchmaking aunt was the last person she wanted to know about Nathan spending the night. "He said he would pick me up around noon. Shall I have him call you then? All right, good-bye."

She began cracking eggs into the mixing bowl, wishing everyone of them was Nathan Hartford's head. He was the most infuriating man. One minute he had her on the verge of tears, the next he made her boiling mad. Let him explain to his aunt where he'd been last night. She had enough trouble with her own mother. Reality had returned with a vengeance.

Everything was ready within a few minutes. Grabbing the silverware in one hand and two place mats in the other, she kept busy by setting the table. The sound of the front door opening stopped her as she headed for the kitchen to get the cups and saucers. It had to be Diane using the extra key. This was the crowning touch of an already insane morning.

"Diane?"

"Oh, Jo, you're up. I called the hospital and George is doing just fine," Diane called back cheerfully as she walked into the dining room. "Darn it, I was going to sneak in and fix us breakfast, but you've started breakfast for us already. You must be a mind reader, or are you?"

The last comment was directed at Nathan, dressed in a pair of jeans and a bath towel slung around his neck. He froze in the middle of the hallway at the sight of Diane.

"Third time's the charm," he said with a shrug, watching Joanna pull a face at him over Diane's head, then he disappeared into the bedroom.

"Wonderful. My plan seems to have done the trick." Diane regarded Joanna closely as her friend began beating the egg mixture furiously.

"Your plan? What are you talking about?" Joanna abandoned the gluttonous mass of pulverized eggs to study Diane's smug smile.

"Getting you and Nathan together for the weekend, that's what." Diane placed her hands on her hips and gave an exaggerated sigh. "The two of you are priceless. He called about you cancelling your picnic plans—which you never told me about—so, I gave him directions to the lake. I thought it was the perfect opportunity to tell him about the baby."

"What baby?"

Neither Joanna nor Diane moved, staring at each other in panic. They didn't want to turn and face the man standing in the hallway behind them.

Joanna closed her eyes, hoping this was a bad dream. In all her seesawing back and forth on how to tell Nathan, this wasn't how she'd imagined it would take place. It was supposed to be a rational, calm discussion about a practical plan on raising their child. She opened her eyes to find Diane still watching her, her blue eyes filled with regret.

Unable to do anything else, she turned to face him. It was as bad as she anticipated. Nathan's hands were clenched at his sides, his eyes dark and brooding as he waited for the answer.

"My baby," she said simply, bracing herself for what else would come.

"I see, so the bacon did make you sick yesterday," he murmured with a decisive nod, his body visibly relaxing as he absorbed her words. Then he took a deep breath before brushing past her to walk into the kitchen.

As she watched open mouthed, he poured a cup of coffee. Pausing a moment, he asked if Diane would like some as well. She nodded dumbly, her startled gaze locking with Joanna's as he poured another cup. He handed Diane her cup before looking at Joanna. "Shall we sit down and discuss this?"

Without taking her eyes off his solemn face, she blindly reached for the back of the nearest chair and sat down, desperately needing the support as her knees suddenly gave out. What was going on behind his unfathomable expression? Had he been thinking about this since yesterday morning, simply waiting for her to explain? She'd left it too late, her apprehension and confusion causing this disaster. It was a calm discussion, but it was too calm.

Nathan pulled out a chair, turning it with a flip of his wrist and straddling it. He rested his forearms on the straight back, holding his cup cradled in his hands as he met Joanna's gaze.

"If you think you're going to marry Collins, and pretend he's the father, think again. I'll be damned if I'll let another man raise my child, especially an idiot like Collins."

Joanna couldn't believe his terse words. This couldn't be coming from the same man who had been dispensing coffee a few minutes ago. Though she marveled that he didn't question the baby was his, she wasn't going to let him dictate to her. She'd been foolish to hold back the information, but she did have a mind of her own.

"It isn't exactly legal for me to marry my own brother," she said quietly. Let him make his demands. She would give him a lesson or two in being blase.

"Your what?" he demanded, slamming his cup down

on the table and ignoring the hot liquid that sloshed on his hand. "Collins is your brother?"

"We were adopted by sisters after our parents were killed."

His arrested look told her that he remembered her words the night before. "I can see why you were so upset last night. I thought the accident made you realize that you loved him more than— Never mind, that isn't important now. Were you planning to tell me that you're carrying my child?"

"Yes, I was going to tell you, but I didn't— I couldn't— I —" she broke off, unable to think of a way to explain. Nothing she could say would sound plausible. She certainly wasn't going to say she'd fallen in love with him and wanted to know his feelings before declaring herself. That was emotional suicide.

"I see. I thought maybe since you've determinedly shut me out of the more important details of your life, I was only being used as a convenient stud service." The last words came out in a low growl, though he still appeared calm. "After all, a trip to Nassau is much more enjoyable than a visit to the sperm bank when the old biological time clock is ticking away."

His bitter words were like a physical blow. She'd been prepared to take the blame for keeping her pregnancy a secret, but she wasn't going to let him insult her. Pushing her hands against the flat surface of the table, she stood up. There was a certain comfort in towering over him with her hands on her hips. "A baby is the last thing I planned on in Nassau. I didn't even plan on having an affair with you; I went there for a vacation to recuperate from the flu. And I wasn't the one that came supplied with a case of those handy, little foil packets, mister. Maybe you shouldn't buy them in bulk the next time, apparently one or two of them were irregulars."

His stunned look gave her a real sense of satisfaction. At the small taste of victory, she forged ahead. "I didn't plan on ever seeing you again. And the day you walked back into my life was the same day I realized I might be pregnant. The next day your uncle innocently told me that you knew exactly who I was when you casually struck up an acquaintance. I didn't think I could trust you, so why would I tell you that I was pregnant?"

"You trusted me enough to sleep with me," he said quietly, "and have me take the responsibility for your protection, though it wasn't good enough."

She didn't have an answer that wouldn't betray how she really felt. Her emotions were raw right now, and she wasn't ready to chance another rebuff. He wasn't giving any hint to how he felt about her or the baby. Oh, he didn't want another man to raise his child, but he didn't say what he planned to do. Though the prospect of motherhood was still new to her, she wasn't going to give up her child, even to the father.

"I'll fight you on this, Nathan. I may not have planned on having a child, but it's mine." If nothing else he would know she was going to stand up for her rights.

"Fine, we'll discuss this again after I've talked to my lawyer," he snapped, getting to his feet. His mouth was set in a grim line as he stalked into the guest room, only to emerge a minute later carrying his suitcase. When he paused for a moment by the table, Joanna refused to look up. "Thanks for the weekend, Joanna."

She waited for the front door to slam before she gave in to her emotions. Too numb to cry, she simply covered her face with her hands, hoping to block out the look of determination that she'd seen on his face before he walked out. Her own fears had led her to this. She was going to have to fight the man she'd fallen in love with for the child neither of them had anticipated.

"Jo, are you all right?"

Diane's voice came as a surprise. Joanna had forgotten about her friend during the encounter with Nathan. The blond was standing at the entrance to the kitchen, looking slightly apprehensive at making her presence known.

"I don't think so, but there isn't anybody to blame but myself," she said in resignation. No matter what the consequences, she should have told Nathan at the beginning. But would it really have made any difference?

"What are you going to do?" Diane came over to sit at the table, reaching out to clasp Joanna's hand.

"I haven't decided yet," she admitted, surprised that she didn't feel anything. But then her body and mind had gone numb the second Nathan asked about the baby. "I've screwed up royally this time. First I fall in love with the arrogant jerk, and now he's going to walk out of my life, just when I was ready to make things right."

"You expected him to, didn't you? I think that's why you've been putting off telling him about the baby. You were afraid to take the chance in case you did lose him."

"What do you mean?" Though she knew the answer, Joanna had to ask the question. She had been hiding from reality too much recently. The reinforcement of a healthy dose of honesty might do her some good.

"The first time you've ever taken a chance at anything was with a stranger on vacation, someone you wouldn't ever see again. But it turned out he wasn't a stranger after all," Diane began slowly, concentrating on selecting each word. "You always play it safe with the men you've dated and whenever any of them started to get serious, you didn't see them again. With Nathan you didn't have that chance; he snuck through your defenses before you realized it."

Joanna absorbed what she was saying, secretly trying to deny it. Unfortunately, Diane had hit too close to the truth. She hadn't wanted to take a chance on losing, even with Nathan. It was always easier to remain detached and be in control of the situation. This time her need to stay in control caused the disaster.

"You've been through enough this morning, without me bothering you with a bunch of psycho-babble," Diane stated, giving Joanna's hand a final squeeze before she stood up. "All I want you to do is think about whether or not you want Nathan in your life. I think the man's in love with you, or he wouldn't have been so hurt about not knowing about the baby. And he was certainly jealous of your brother.

"Right now, though, I'm going to fix you and my future god-child some breakfast before we go visit George," she said with her usual good humor. "You go wash your face and get ready. Things will look better after you've had a chance to recover from the shock."

Joanna didn't say a word, because she didn't share Diane's optimistic outlook. Not telling Nathan about the baby was undoubtedly the biggest mistake in her life, and she was going to pay for it.

"There you are, son. I was beginning to get worried."

Evan's voice stayed Nathan's hand as he fit the plastic card into the door lock of his hotel room. With a glance at the older man, he put the card in and twisted the door handle. "Morning, Evan."

"Helen's about to send out a search party since she couldn't track you down at Joanna's over an hour ago," Evan continued as he followed Nathan into his room. "I finally decided to check your room one more time before she called the police."

Nathan tossed his suitcase on the bed and shrugged out of his jacket. He needed the time to come up with a more plausible story than his aimless driving around town after he left Joanna's apartment. Unfortunately his brain was preoccupied with the same problem. How was he going to repair the damage he'd done this morning? The image of Joanna's set face haunted him.

"I was too tired to drive back here last night, so I bunked down in the car," he stated, going to open the drapes. Movement seemed to help him think. The bright sunlight hurt his eyes, but he needed some kind of stimulation to keep functioning. "I went to the hospital to check on George, then I called," he hesitated over the word as he opened his suitcase, "Joanna. She was already planning on going to the hospital with Diane, so I decided to come back here to clean up and get some sleep in a decent bed."

"Well, your aunt's going to be very disappointed," the older man murmured, lowering himself into the arm chair by the window.

Nathan looked up from unpacking his suitcase, only mildly interested in Evan's words. Everything else in the world was trivial compared to the hurt he'd inflicted on Joanna this morning. He'd been a pompous idiot letting his pride overcome his common sense this morning.

"Yes, Helen was sure she'd finally managed to find your match," Evan went on as if Nathan's silence was as normal as the man putting his shoes in the drawer. "You'd better watch your step, that woman is determined to get you married off, by fair means or foul."

"She's probably going to have a long wait," Nathan returned before tossing his shirt into the drawer of the armoire. Unless he managed to repair the damage he'd done this morning, he wouldn't be marrying anyone, not if he couldn't have Joanna. "Now, I hate to throw you out, but I've got to get some sleep."

"No problem. You'd better get some rest while you can. With Collins out of action, we've got some major reorganizing to do to keep the Washington project on schedule." Evan got to his feet and walked to Nathan's side. He met the younger man's gaze in the mirror over the desk before clamping a hand on his shoulder. "We'll talk later."

For a moment Nathan stared at his own bleak reflection. He was surprised to discover only the bluish shadows of fatigue under his eyes, instead of the signs of twenty years of aging. He certainly felt it inside. Meeting the image of his uncle's almost identical gray eyes in the glass, he asked, "Did you know that Collins is Joanna's brother?"

A rueful smile curved the older man's lips before he squeezed his nephew's shoulder again and dropped his hand to his side. "So you finally found that out, did you?"

"How did you know?" he exclaimed, turning to the other man in surprise. Evan's question finally jolted him out of his lethargy.

"It wasn't exactly a secret. Collins listed her as his beneficiary on his health insurance," his uncle explained, his smile broadening into a wide grin. "You should read the personnel files more often. Insurance forms ask for a beneficiary and the relationship to the employee."

He regarded his uncle with narrowed eyes, his mind replaying snatches of conversations over the past few weeks. "Helen isn't the only one who's been playing matchmaker."

Evan didn't try to deny the statement and simply shrugged. "I've always told you that something worth having, is something that has to be won. That's why we work so well together. I've never given you anything that you haven't worked hard to attain.

"Now, I need to tell Helen that you've turned up safe and sound. Pleasant dreams."

Nathan stared after his uncle, bemused at the man's statement. Would Evan be so supportive if he knew what a mess his nephew had made of his life lately? He mulled over the conversation as he automatically undressed and headed for the shower. The bracing rush of water finally roused him out of his reflections.

Evan was right. No man deserved a reward unless he was willing to work hard for it, Nathan determined as he toweled his damp body. Now that his mind was working, he realized that he was going to fight Joanna. Not for custody of the baby, but for her love. He wasn't going to let her turn her back on the future they could have together.

He wasn't sure how he was going to do it, or how long it would take, but he was going to marry Joanna. As he climbed into bed, he hoped that their kid wasn't going to be graduating from college by the time his or her stubborn parents had managed to walk down the aisle.

"Will I live, Doc?" George asked in a whisper as the doctor straightened and adjusted the stethoscope around his neck.

"Unfortunately, you'll be around to plague me quite a few years, young man," Dr. Dreyer said, managing a slight smile from his patient, "but you were lucky this time. I'd think twice about passing a sleepy truck driver on a wet road after this."

"I second that, wholeheartedly," came Joanna's voice from her chair in the corner as the doctor wrote on George's chart.

"Oh, Jo, I'm so sorry you had to be put through this." George rolled his head across his pillow and put out his hand to his sister. "Hope you didn't have those nightmares again."

"No, sweetie, they didn't bother me at all," she assured him, and gave his hand a reassuring squeeze. She knew he sometimes felt guilty that he never remembered much about his early childhood, but he'd been four when their parents were killed. "It was a shock when Diane called, but I managed." She didn't dwell on the details, more for her own peace of mind than to comfort him.

"Kept thinking about you worrying last night. Glad I didn't have a wife and kids, but didn't want you to worry," he murmured, shutting his eyes as he squeezed her hand again.

Joanna looked across the bed at the doctor, trying to see if he was worried about George's ramblings. Dr. Dreyer gave her an encouraging smile. "He's a little groggy from his medication. It's perfectly normal. He's been preoccupied about not letting anybody worry about him since he came around the first time.

"Let's go out in the hall. He's going to be sleeping on and off most of the day," the doctor continued, walking around the end of the bed. "You can come back tonight for another visit. And don't waste any time worrying, he'll be on his feet by the end of the week."

Joanna was still thinking about George's words after the doctor said good-bye. The accident had shaken him. What disturbed her the most was the connection to what Diane had said earlier. Had both of them subconsciously avoided commitment because of the tragedy in their childhood? Had it made that much an impression to effect their lives? She avoided all intimate relationships, and George had a succession of women in his life, none of them lasting longer than a few months.

Well, George was wrong about one thing, she thought as she entered the waiting room a few minutes later. She smiled in answer to Diane's anxious look. There were others who were worried about him.

"He's gone to sleep again," she said as Diane got to her feet. "The doctor said we can come back later tonight, but why don't you go take a peek in his room before we leave.''

Diane flashed her a grateful smile and hurried out of the room. Joanna followed at a slower pace, wondering how she was going to get through the rest of the day. Sitting at home brooding didn't appeal to her. The sight of a couple getting off the elevator carrying flowers and an arm load of wrapped packages gave her an inspiration.

She and Diane would go shopping. She had a great deal to accomplish before her baby made an appearance. The guest room had to be redecorated and baby furniture had to be picked out. What did babies need for clothes besides diapers? Joanna didn't have the faintest idea. She'd always bought toys for shower gifts in the past.

There was also the question of her own wardrobe, she decided, looking down at the straight skirt she was wearing. Had it been her imagination that the waist was a little tighter than usual this morning? She needed to discover if there was such a term as fashion in maternity clothing. Did they make business suits for pregnant women?

"George looks about ten years old when he's asleep,'' Diane announced as she joined Joanna near the nurse's station.

"What do you know about baby clothes?''

Joanna's question erased the dreamy smile from the blond's lips. She narrowed her eyes, before saying tentatively, "They're small.''

"Oh, this is going to be an interesting afternoon, Auntie Di.'' Joanna chuckled as she linked arms with the other woman and lead her toward the elevator. "We're going on an afternoon mission to explore a strange new world called Babyland.''

Diane looked skeptical as they stepped into the elevator. "Joanna, are you all right? There's a strange gleam in your eye.''

"I'm recovering, slowly but surely," she answered and was surprised that she was telling the truth. Going shopping for the baby's things was giving her an incredible lift, like a shot of adrenaline. She was dealing with the reality of her life, and it wasn't so bad.

This was the first step. This was establishing the permanency of the baby in her life. She'd get over the easy ground before she tackled the next, more difficult step. It was more than a step, it was a hurdle.

Reestablishing communication with the baby's father would be difficult, but Joanna made her living at solving problems and attracting people's attention. Nathan might be the toughest campaign she'd ever tackled. However, it was a project that would be challenging and worth the effort.

TEN

"Good morning, Diane. Would you care to join me for one of these nutritious cranberry muffins? There's some for you and the rest of the troops, too, Anita," Joanna announced as she strolled through the front doors of Trent-Barringer the next morning. Both Anita and Diane gave her a puzzled look as she plopped a bakery box down on the desk. "Why are you both looking so gloomy? It's a gorgeous spring day and the beginning of a new week."

"Don't worry about this, Anita. I think the lack of caffeine is waking up some dormant brain cells," Diane whispered to the confused secretary. "I don't think she's dangerous, but I'll take her into her office and keep her out of sight, just the same."

"Was that a nasty crack?" Joanna asked, opening the box and taking out two muffins.

"In the four years I've known you, I've never seen you this cheerful before noon," Diane stated and followed Joanna into her office, closing the door firmly behind her. "You're borderline perky, as a matter of fact, which tells me that you're planning something, or have gotten too much sugar in your diet lately."

"I should be insulted, but unfortunately, you have a point. However, I'm not on a sugar high," she answered,

171

walking into the kitchenette without expanding on the statement. After picking up a handful of napkins and taking a bottle of apple juice from the refrigerator, she turned to find Diane blocking the doorway. "Did you want to eat in here? I thought the couch would be more comfortable."

"Damn, I hate it when you're being enigmatic," the other woman snapped, but stepped out of the way. "What happened to that fairly solemn creature that dragged me through every furniture and clothing store at three malls yesterday?"

"She did some thinking last night, and she's tired of watching life from the sidelines," she explained. Diane followed her to the couch and sat down without saying a word while Joanna poured herself a glass of apple juice. "As of this morning, she's going to be an active participant."

"Is this supposed to make sense?"

"You should know, my friend, since you're the one who's inspired this idea." Joanna sat back and crossed her legs, trying to draw out the explanation. She wasn't sure how Diane was going to react to what she had in mind. But if she presented it the right way, maybe her friend wouldn't have too many objections.

"Jo, this is driving me nuts. What idea?"

"You said I was running away from being emotionally involved, right?"

"Well, yes, but what does that—"

"Just bear with me on this. Yesterday George said something curious about not having a wife and kids to worry over his accident." She was getting close to the tricky area and wanted Diane's complete involvement. "Last night I thought about what you said as well as George. Then I began analyzing my behavior since I met Nathan. I realized that getting pregnant was one of the best things that could have happened to me."

"I think I'm going to need some coffee for this," Diane

muttered, getting up to retrieve her cup from the outer office. "This is the weirdest thing I've ever heard."

She came back a minute later, alternately shaking her head and taking a sip from her cup. "It's not helping. Run this by me again."

"My affair in Nassau was emotionally safe, giving my emotions a free reign without having to worry about losing Nathan in the future. It wasn't that I was tired of being too practical and too responsible all the time. Until the other night I hadn't realized that I'd subconsciously avoided any emotional involvement. I thought I didn't trust Nathan, but I didn't trust myself," she continued, wishing she could have some of Diane's coffee. This was harder to explain than she anticipated. "Any way, to get to the point. I've lost important people in my life that I love, and I didn't want to face that hurt again, even if it is part of living. But now, I'm going to take a gamble on being hurt to get what I want out of life. I'm not letting Nathan Hartford walk out of my life without a fight."

"All right, Joanna," Diane exclaimed, starting to her feet, but stopped with a look at her friend's anxious expression. She sat down again on the edge of the couch, and asked suspiciously, "What are you planning to do?"

"I'm going to find out whether he loves me or not," she said with a decisive nod. "And to do that I need the name of your friend who practices family law."

"Why do you need Eileen's help?"

"She's going to write up a custody and financial agreement for me. Nathan said he was planning to see a lawyer, and I think it's a good idea for opening communications between us."

"I hate to say this, but I think you're making sense," Diane said after a moment's consideration. Cocking her head to the side, she studied her friend. "Just promise me that you aren't going to get carried away with this document."

"Of course not, that's why I want a lawyer. This will help both Nathan and me meet again without sacrificing our pride," Joanna responded, hoping that she didn't look terribly guilty. The document was the key to her strategy. It would have to be fairly stringent on Nathan's limitation to custody, so he would react.

"All right, I'll go call Eileen now to set up an appointment," Diane agreed. She got up and walked to the door, still pondering the situation.

Once the door closed behind her partner, Joanna let her shoulders sag in relief. She'd managed to convince Diane, so maybe it wasn't such a harebrained scheme after all. It had sounded so reasonable last night around two in the morning. This morning, however, she'd been plagued with doubts.

Nathan was attracted to her, and he'd been hurt by her secretiveness over the baby. That didn't necessarily add up to love. There were moments she thought it was only wishful thinking on her part that she imagined he felt anything stronger than passion. But Diane thought he loved her, and there was something she'd remembered last night that she hoped was an omen. Something Nathan began to say in the heat of the moment yesterday.

I thought the accident made you realize you loved him more than— She was gambling on the chance he'd thought she loved George more than him. That could only matter to him if he was in love with her, and she hoped she was gambling on a sure thing and not a hundred to one shot.

"Where have you been? Visiting hours started forty-five minutes ago," George complained as soon as Joanna entered his hospital room the following evening. He was not being a model patient after being confined to bed almost seventy-two hours.

"My, aren't we cheerful. I see your disposition hasn't

improved since yesterday," she returned sweetly. Her tolerance wasn't helped by the fact he was on his best behavior whenever anyone else was in the room, especially Diane, and he reverted to a spoiled brat when Joanna was alone.

"How would you like to lie here with nothing to do but change the channels on the TV set?"

"Right now it sounds like heaven after a long day at work," she answered honestly. "I thought you'd at least be glad you're back on solid food."

"The food hasn't improved any."

"Neither has your attitude," Joanna muttered. She knew that she was being overly sensitive today, but she was nervous after her appointment with Eileen Korbel. The custody agreement was tucked in her purse, ready to be delivered. Looking around the room, she decided to try for a better bedside manner. "Who sent the dark orange mums? They're lovely."

"Diane sent them this morning," he said tonelessly, then frowned. "Where is she any way? She said she would bring me some cookies tonight."

"She didn't remember she had a date until it was too late to cancel. Paul had tickets to something, so she'll bring the cookies tomorrow," she told him as casually as possible, watching his reaction with interest. Hopefully someone's romance might be going smoother than her own.

"Not Paul Stanley again?" he practically snarled. "Doesn't she have any sense? That man's a menace."

"Oh, come on, George. What have you got against him?" She tried to keep from grinning as his lower lip came out in a pout. Too bad she didn't have a video camera for this performance. Diane would love it. "I've only met him twice, but he seems no different from any other red-blooded, single male. No better, no worse."

"Humph!"

"Okay, buster, since you want to be entertained, what do you want to do? A game of cut throat scrabble or maybe some gin rummy?" Joanna asked in hopes of lightening both their moods. Playing a game would keep her mind off her own problems and manage to keep George from getting too restless.

"I guess—Nathan, you made it."

Joanna froze in her chair, but she could see the tall figure in the doorway in her peripheral vision. What was he doing here?

What an idiot. You didn't think about her being here. Or were you hoping she would be? He took a slow, measured step into the room. Joanna wasn't looking at him. That wasn't good. "I finally made it past the dragon lady at the nurse's station, thanks to the note Dr. Dreyer left behind," Nathan explained, relieved his voice didn't crack. Counting to ten he turned his head. "Hello, Joanna. I hope I haven't come at a bad time."

It would have been better if I'd had some warning, she answered silently before straightening in her chair. "Not really. We were just going to play cards to keep George from climbing the walls," *which I'll probably be doing in a few minutes myself, if my nerves snap.* She was glad her voice came out in a normal tone. As she looked up to meet his gaze, she tried not to stare; her heartbeat seemed lodged in her throat. He looked so good in his tan suit. "What's this about a dragon lady?"

"Nathan's taking over the Washington project temporarily," her brother explained to her disappointment, making Joanna look at him instead of the silent man standing at the end of the bed. "The head nurse wouldn't let him in the room with his briefcase yesterday. So, I talked to Dr. Dreyer this morning, and had him write out a permission slip."

Does she look more beautiful than ever tonight, or is it

my imagination? "The lady wasn't too happy about it, but it was sweet revenge for yesterday when she threatened to frisk me," Nathan admitted with a slight smile, reaching up to brush his index finger over his mustache as he dared to glance at Joanna again. *I wouldn't have turned you down.*

I don't blame her, Joanna decided with a sigh. She also wanted to get a look at this woman, and warn her off if necessary. Nathan was hers, even if he didn't know yet.

"Jo, you don't mind if we get to this, do you? I'm glad you came, but—"

"But you have men's work to do, and the little lady will just be in the way," she finished for him, not offended by his blatant invitation to leave. Trust George to be oblivious to everything, but his work, she thought affectionately as she dared another look at Nathan from beneath her lashes. She only regretted she couldn't sit quietly in the corner to watch Nathan, then realized how silly it sounded—even to herself. *I've got it bad.*

"Really, Joanna, I don't want to run you off," Nathan said earnestly. *I'd rather have you right here next to me all night.* Damn, but he couldn't think of a single reason for her stay.

She smiled at him, hugging his concerned expression to her heart. He actually seemed disappointed that she was leaving. It was a good sign. "Don't worry. I know engineers too well. In a few minutes, you won't remember I'm here. I'll leave before I have to compete with your tunnel plans."

Nothing would make me forget you, Nathan pledged, but couldn't think of a single word to say aloud as he watched her walk to the door.

"Don't forget to remind Diane about the cookies," her brother called as she reached the doorway.

"I won't," she returned with a short laugh, clutching

her purse to her side. She looked directly at Nathan for one last time, hoping she appeared casual when she asked, "When are you leaving for Washington?"

"Tomorrow night, if I get everything cleared away on the Chicago project tomorrow." *Too damn soon to make up for being such an ass on Sunday.*

"Well, have a good trip." She walked out before she did or said anything to give away her agitation. There were only twenty-four hours to put her plan into effect. How was she going to manage it? She didn't think she could hand it to him herself. So, how was it going to be done?

How was he going to get Joanna back when he was halfway across the country? Nathan thought desperately as he began pulling papers out of his briefcase. George was nattering away about the blasting technique, but he didn't care. His heart wasn't in the project; it had just gone out the door with a certain gorgeous brunette.

And more importantly, she was speaking to him, had even smiled at him. He'd anticipated their next meeting being awkward and chilly. Maybe it was the unexpectedness of their meeting, but he didn't think so. Joanna was relaxed in his company. The thought gave him real hope. Tonight he might rest easier, instead of lying awake trying to rehearse the conversation on how to apologize to her.

"Well, are you going to show it to me or not?" Diane demanded over lunch the next day. She was practically bouncing up and down in her chair.

"Show you what?" Joanna asked innocently, knowing exactly what Diane was talking about as she smoothed her napkin over her navy print skirt. Luckily her partner had been busy with a production layout most of the morning, and didn't have time to ask too many questions before now.

"Joanna, come on—"

"Did I remind you about George's cookies?" she interrupted. She'd read the document a hundred times last night and was beginning to waver. Was it really a good idea, or would she be antagonizing Nathan unnecessarily? Maybe this wasn't such a good time to establish her emotional independence.

"No, you didn't, but it doesn't matter since I already baked them before I remembered my date with Paul."

"Oh, George wasn't exactly pleased about that either." She dug into her pasta salad with enthusiasm. Her appetite had increased ten fold in the past few days. "You know I might have to do some serious shopping for maternity clothes soon."

"Serious shopping? What was that marathon we did on Sunday? A practice run?" Diane put down her fork deliberately and leaned against the table. "Now, give me a straight answer on this, without any nonsense about George being jealous of Paul Stanley. Are you going to let me see that document, or not?"

"Well, he was jealous. He said, 'Doesn't she have any sense? The man's a menace,' " she mimicked in a fairly good impersonation of her brother. "It was really cute when he pouted, too, over not getting his cookies. Too bad Nathan interrupted—"

"Oh, good Lord, you haven't given it to him already," Diane exclaimed, becoming more agitated, not noticing the stares of the people at the neighboring table.

"You're really worried about this, if George can't distract you," Joanna murmured and leaned down to pick up her purse, giving in to the inevitable. It would probably help to have Diane read over the agreement and get a somewhat objective opinion. Eileen Korbel had been pleased with the result, but she was used to reading dry, contorted legalese.

"You can tell me every detail about George later. Right now I want to hear about Nathan."

"I almost fell out of my chair when he walked in the door," Joanna admitted, trying to analyze the meeting from a new perspective. "It wasn't much, but it wasn't terrible either."

"Oh, that tells me a lot," Diane complained.

"We talked to each other like I was George's sister and he was George's boss—the usual Hello-how-are-you-how-nice-to-see-you-again. He smiled twice," she finished with a smile of her own.

"Oh, that's good."

"It would be, if he wasn't leaving for Washington tonight," Joanna declared, suddenly losing her appetite. She still hadn't thought of a way to give Nathan the custody agreement. Now she wasn't sure it would have the right impact, since he wouldn't be in St. Louis to complete the plan.

"What are you going to do about that tricky little piece of paper?"

"I haven't decided. Here, go ahead and read it. Maybe you can think of a good plan." Chewing on her lower lip, she handed Diane the folded pieces of paper. Suddenly she didn't know what to do with her hands as she waited for her friend to read through the document.

It was fairly straightforward. Nathan wasn't asked for any financial support, but was given visitation rights. The one clause that was a little extreme concerned what would happen if Joanna married. According to the agreement, Nathan would have to agree to the child's adoption by Joanna's husband, if that was what the unknown man wanted to do.

A sharp whistle from across the table told her exactly what part of the document Diane was reading. "Oh, Joanna, you'll be lucky he doesn't rip this into tiny, little pieces. It should certainly do the trick, especially with him going out of town."

"You think I should give it to him then?" she asked anxiously, still not used to the emotional merry-go-round. One minute she was sure this was what needed to be done; the next she wanted to return to her safe cocoon.

"As much as I hate to admit it, yes," Diane agreed without hesitation. "It's not terribly conventional, but you certainly can't say that this has been a normal romance. When you decide to take a chance, you really pull out all the stops."

"But do you think it will work?" She was desperate for reassurance, which didn't help her frame of mind. Before she'd met Nathan her self-confidence had never faltered. Now she seemed to question every move she made, every word she said.

"Take it easy, hon." Diane laughed as she handed the papers back. "I think I'm beginning to envy you. My biggest ambition right now is trying to get a date with your brother."

"At least you know where he's going to be for the next few weeks," Joanna said with a resigned sigh, absently picking up a piece of celery to munch on.

"That's true, but that ankle to thigh cast isn't going to further anybody's romance."

"He can't run away."

"Cute," Diane replied dryly. "Okay, back to Nathan. We need to come up with an idea on how to give him the custody agreement."

"If we're lucky, it might even be before the baby's born," Joanna murmured, and bit off another piece of celery.

"Wait a minute, I think I've got it."

* * *

"Joanna, this is a delightful surprise," Evan Hartford exclaimed as his secretary ushered Joanna into his office two hours later.

"I'd finished revising your entertainment schedule after Nathan gave me the latest changes. I had an appointment down the street, so I thought I'd drop it off personally," she explained in a rush as she shook his hand. *Diane and her brilliant ideas,* she thought wildly, *I can't grill Evan about Nathan's work schedule.*

"You must be a mind reader, because I was just about to give you a call," he told her, waving her into the arm chair in front of his glass and chrome desk.

"Not another change?"

"You can relax. I need to ask a favor for my wife," he continued. He gave her a sheepish smile as he returned to the chair behind his desk. "I've set up a meeting tonight with a new client and have created a major problem. Helen is flying home tonight."

"And you'd like me to drive her to the airport," she finished for him.

"It would be a big help. She hates hotel limos and—"

"Evan, I'll be glad to do it," she broke in, hating to see him look so uncomfortable over the request. "It will give me a chance to see her before she leaves. I'm sorry I haven't been able to arrange another day to get together after we had such a good time in St. Charles."

"I can't say the same after I got a look at my checkbook," he admitted, his twinkling eyes contradicting his complaint. "She'll be delighted with the arrangement. Let me give her a quick call."

Joanna shifted nervously in her chair, her fingers plucking at a loose thread in the seam of her briefcase. How was she going to manage this? First she'd give Evan the revised schedule—that was easy—but, then she had to give him a sealed envelope for Nathan as if it was an everyday occurrence. *Oh, it's nothing, Evan, just a little legal matter between me and your nephew. Certainly nothing that you'd be interested in seeing.*

"That's settled then," Evan stated as he hung up the receiver. "Helen's delighted. She'll be ready about seven."

"I'm so glad I could help," she murmured, and for one insane moment, considered throwing herself on Evan's mercy. But dismissed the thought immediately. She had to handle this herself.

"Evan, here's my final report—" Nathan broke off when he looked up from the paper in his hand to look directly into Joanna's startled face. "Sorry to interrupt. Bernice wasn't at her guard desk, so I didn't know you were busy."

"No problem, I was just about to leave," Joanna managed to get out around the lump in her throat. She stood up, hoping her legs would hold as Nathan stopped a foot away. "I just dropped off the revised entertainment schedule while I was in the neighborhood."

"What was that about a report, Nathan?"

"This is the Chicago report and my Washington schedule. I'll be able to leave tonight after all."

Joanna took a deep swallow as Nathan's fathomless gaze never wavered from her face as he spoke to his uncle. There wasn't any way she was going to be able to give him the legal papers in front of his uncle. Damn.

"Terrific, your plane leaves about twenty minutes before Helen's flight," Evan said as he glanced over the itinerary Nathan handed him. "If you ask nicely, maybe Joanna will give you a lift to the airport, since she's agreed to take your aunt."

Nathan was afraid to move, or even speak. This was too good to be true. He'd spent most of the morning with his hand hovering over the telephone, trying to think of an excuse to call Joanna. Even if he couldn't arrange to see her before he left, he could hear her voice.

"Well, Nathan, how does that sound?" his uncle prompted.

"Oh, sorry, I was trying to remember my schedule," he answered absently, then cleared his throat. "I have a call coming in at six, but I should be ready to leave by seven. Is that convenient for you, Joanna?"

"It's perfect."

Nathan let out his pent up breath, but didn't completely relax. He didn't know how to interpret her hesitant smile. There was so much he wanted to say, to reassure her, only not with his uncle hovering over them. Would he have any better chance tonight with Helen in tow?

"Well, gentlemen, I need to get back to work," Joanna exclaimed with a glance at the wall clock. She smiled at Evan and gave Nathan a slight nod before turning and hurrying out of the office.

"Well, are you going to thank me or not?" Evan demanded before the door clicked shut behind Joanna's departing figure.

Nathan roused himself from his thoughts, and turned to look at the older man. "For what? If you were really in top form, you wouldn't have stuck me with a chaperon."

"Nobody's perfect," he answered with a shrug. "Think how much more interesting it will be with a third person eavesdropping on every syllable."

"Still making me work for the prize, I see," Nathan murmured with a reluctant smile, shaking his head as he walked out of his uncle's office. Maybe it wouldn't be so bad with a first class matchmaker along. After all, Joanna had a moderately sized sedan, and Helen could sit in comfort in the back seat, alone. All he had to manage was an apology and a proposal in the short drive to the airport.

"Are you by yourself?" George asked in surprise as Diane entered his room that evening. He watched her move across the room, absently pushing his glasses back in place with his index finger.

"Um-hmmm, Joanna had to stop by the Jackson Foundation cocktail party; they've been complaining about the caterer. She might stop by before she takes the Hartfords out to the airport," she explained as she walked over to the bed. Was he still irritated about her date last night, or was he simply bored?

"Did you bring me something?" he inquired hopefully, dismissing his sister as he spotted the large canvas tote bag that was looped over Diane's arm.

"You sound like a little kid," she chided him lightly. Her pulse was beating double time as she stood watching his scowling face. Was this the face of a jealous man? Joanna was nuts; George just missed his cookies. "Will chocolate chip cookies and a jigsaw puzzle satisfy you?"

"That'll do," he mumbled. Then he hesitated a moment, picking at the top of the sheet and ducking his head before peering up at her over the top of his glasses. "The cookies are a little late, aren't they?"

"Yes, they are," Diane answered a little breathlessly. Maybe Joanna wasn't nuts after all. She could feel her cheeks start to burn under his intense turquoise gaze before he became interested in the sheet again. "Joanna said you were put out last night." She looked at his bent head for a few minutes before she spoke. "What have you got against me dating Paul Stanley?"

"Oh, nothing really," he grumbled without looking up. "I just don't have much to look forward to while I'm laying around here. I like having company."

"Is there any reason I shouldn't go out with him?" she persisted. If Joanna could stick her neck out, so could she.

George wished he'd never brought up the subject. He sounded like a spoiled child, which wasn't the impression he was trying to make. "He's, um, he's not trustworthy."

"Trustworthy? George, that's ridiculous. Going out with Paul isn't any riskier than going out with . . . with you," Diane exclaimed, trying not to laugh at his brotherly statement. "From what I've heard, you're no babe in the woods."

"Oh, for God's sake," he shot back, his expression outraged as he snapped his head up. "I didn't want to start an argument. And how would you know what I'm like, you've never gone out with me." His voice rose to match hers, not really paying attention to what he said.

"You never asked me," she replied quickly, amazed at how well this was going, "so how would I know. Anyway, those floozies you constantly have hanging all over you, aren't exactly girl scouts. They're more like the kind that get paid for their time."

"That's ridiculous. I've never had to pay for companionship," he snapped, rising awkwardly to a sitting position. "And why should I ask you out? You'd only turn me down."

"How do you know I would? You never bothered, except for lunch now and then."

"So, who wants to date their friend's little brother?" he asked bitterly. "Just give him a sweet smile and a pat on the head occasionally, that should keep him happy. Dear, little George; he's such a sweetie, but dreadfully absentminded, so be patient with him," he barely ground out between clenched teeth, letting out all the frustrations that had built up over the few days of inactivity.

"I'll show you who's absentminded." He took hold of her wrist and began pulling her toward him. "I'm twenty-seven years old, not ten, and this should prove it."

"George, you're letting your temper get out of hand." Diane put up a token resistance, careful to keep from jarring his leg, but curious about what he intended to do. Her curiosity was quickly rewarded. With one tug on her wrist, he pulled her across his chest and captured her parted lips. She took full advantage of what could be the only opportunity to be in this delightful situation. As the embrace lengthened, she was in complete agreement with George. He certainly wasn't that absentminded, and no ten-year-old ever kissed like this.

George suddenly realized what he was doing, though his anger had been replaced by other, more pleasant, emotions. Groaning at his insane impulse, he pulled away from the delight of Diane's lips. He framed her flushed face between his trembling hands. "Diane, I'm sorry," he apologized softly, terribly unsure of himself without understanding why. Her face was slightly out of focus, and he realized that his glasses had come off sometime in the last few minutes. "I didn't mean to take out my temper on you. It's no excuse, but being confined to bed is damned frustrating."

"Are you sorry you lost your temper, or are you sorry you kissed me?" she barely whispered, lowering her eyes to the hem of the sheet. "Was kissing me that unpleasant?" she continued in a rush, breaking into a teasing smile. "I rather enjoyed it."

"You did?" He wondered if he was dreaming. If it was a dream, he wanted it to continue indefinitely. For weeks he'd been wondering how to get her to take him seriously, actually see him as a man, not Joanna's brother. "So did I."

"Then why don't we try it again, now that neither of us is angry," she suggested, raising her lashes in time to see his worried expression break into a broad grin.

"Not a bad idea," he agreed, proceeding with the experiment.

ELEVEN

"That was much better, wasn't it?" Diane sighed a few minutes later as she nestled her head in the curve of his shoulder.

"Diane? How long does it take to fall in love?"

"I don't know," she answered contentedly, her eyes closed as she listened to his erratic heartbeat. "I've only done it once."

"Only once?" he asked anxiously as his arms tightened around her. "What was he like?"

"You tell me," she demanded, raising her head to look into his worried eyes, holding her breath as she waited for his answer.

"Me? That's impossible," he argued without much conviction, and wondered why he was contradicting her. He had to be dreaming. Any second now he would wake up to unpleasant reality. "You've known me for years and never gave a sign of having any interest in me."

"And what would you have done if I had? Probably run in the opposite direction," she accused with a laugh. Encouraged by the fact he still held her firmly in his arms, she raised her hand to run her fingers caressingly down his cheek. "Why did you want to know about falling in love? Does it have something to do with kissing me?"

"Because I love you, of course," he stated firmly, a startled look crossing his face at the revelation. "All this time I've been jealous of Paul and any one else you dated. You aren't going to see him anymore.'"

"Why shouldn't I?" she inquired with an innocent look.

"The woman who marries me doesn't date other men," he replied with authority.

"Am I going to marry you?"

"You are," he said in the same decisive tone, before adding, "I hope."

"If that's a proposal, I'm accepting while you're still in a helpless position," she answered unsteadily. "Once you're out of the hospital, you might find something to distract you."

"You mean someone, don't you? Possibly one of my paid companions?" He chuckled as she flushed over the slur to his character. "You're going to pay for that one."

"How?" she asked provocatively, raising her lips within an inch of his.

"How about this?" he murmured as he accepted her invitation.

They lost themselves in whispered endearments and reassurances, shutting out the rest of the world. The sound of Joanna's voice from the hallway was like a blast of cold water, bringing them back to the real world.

"Is this any way to treat a sick man?" Joanna demanded from the doorway. Since the orderly was coming down the hall to retrieve the dinner trays, she thought she should give the embracing couple on the bed a chance to collect themselves.

"Oh, hi, Jo," her brother called, giving her a fatuous smile as Diane scrambled to her feet.

"Ah, George liked the cookies," Diane muttered as she

tried to brush the wrinkles out of her linen skirt, but it was difficult. George wouldn't let go of her hand.

"So I guessed," Joanna returned, trying not to laugh. George suddenly realized he wasn't wearing his glasses and was frantically patting the sheets with his free hand. "Should I ask if your intentions are honorable, Ms. Barringer?"

"Joanna," her friend gasped and blushed a brilliant red just as the orderly walked through the door.

"We're getting married," her brother announced as he set his glasses on his nose with an air of satisfaction. "How about next week, sweetheart?"

"What?" Diane and Joanna exclaimed in two part harmony.

"Well, why not? I'll be on sick leave when they release me from this joint, so why not go ahead and get married?" he asked, looking from his sister to his new fiancée, not understanding their consternation.

"How did this happen?" Joanna finally managed to ask, looking at Diane for a reasonable explanation.

"I took a chance, and it worked," Diane stated, still stunned by the results of her challenge to George. "I just followed your example."

"Well, I hope my luck is as good as yours," she murmured in return, her head going automatically to her purse. In about a half hour she was going to give Nathan the custody agreement. Shaking off a feeling of dread, she forced a smile on her face. Her brother's and best friend's engagement deserved her full attention, she decided, as she hugged Diane. "Congratulations. I hope you know what you're getting yourself into by marrying my brother."

"Hey, I'm an invalid, remember? Be nice."

Joanna bent over to kiss his cheek. "Maybe a wedding

with you in a cast isn't such a bad idea. At least she'll have your undivided attention for about six weeks."

"You have a point," Diane murmured as she perched on the side of the bed, a contented smile on her face as George put his arm around her waist.

"Are you two still going to gang up on me all the time?" he asked with a frown. "That doesn't seem fair."

"Well, I'll leave you two alone for now, and Diane can make up for our abuse. I've got to go pick up my passengers at the hotel."

"Good luck," Diane called after her as she hurried out the door.

"She's just going to the airport," Joanna heard her brother say as she rounded the corner.

Yes, she was *just* going to the airport. A trip that could determine her future. Maybe George and Diane's engagement was a good omen. Her friend had taken a chance and her gamble had paid off. Would she be as fortunate with Nathan?

"Here's your magazines, Helen," Nathan announced as he walked up to the two women standing in line at the departure gate.

"Oh, Nathan, you're an angel," his aunt exclaimed, her gratitude making him feel guilty for his dark thoughts on the ride to the airport.

He'd been late meeting them at the hotel, and Helen was already sitting in the front seat of the car. Watching Joanna's profile during the ride to the airport was gratifying, but there wasn't a chance to have a personal conversation. Now he only had a few minutes left.

"Nathan, you'd better get to your gate. Evan would never let me hear the end of it if you missed your flight," Helen exclaimed, oblivious to her companions' silence as their eyes met over her head. "Oh, no. There's the boarding call now."

"Joanna." He tried to think of something, anything before he left. But what?

"I have something I've been meaning to give you," she said in a breathless voice, holding an envelope in front of her. The white rectangle was creased and battered looking, as if she'd been carrying it for quite a while.

He reached for it automatically, hesitating for a moment when he noticed her trembling hand. Why did she look so distressed? She was nibbling on her lower lip, her eyes a vivid green that told him her emotions were highly charged. He wanted to take her in his arms and comfort her, but didn't know the cause for her anxiety. Was she sorry that he was going?

"Oh, for heaven's sakes, Nathan, are you going to kiss her or not?" his aunt asked impatiently as he took a step forward. "Make up your mind, before you miss your plane."

He snapped his head in his aunt's direction, and she winked at him. What did he have to lose? He couldn't repress a smile of anticipation as he took a startled Joanna in his arms. This was the way it was meant to be, he thought as Joanna's lips parted beneath his. This was what he should have done Sunday, instead of losing his temper. He'd been a fool.

A minute later he was striding down the concourse as Joanna stood in a daze, her hand to her lips. She wanted to run after him, and grab the envelope that he still held clutched in his hand.

"Joanna, are you all right?"

Everyone is always asking me that, Joanna thought wildly as she looked down at Helen's concerned face. She had to get hold of herself if she was going to be in any condition to drive home. However, she could still feel the electricity of Nathan's all too brief kiss in her blood stream.

"You aren't angry with me, are you?"

"Angry? Why should I be angry?" Joanna asked, bewildered by the question.

"Never mind, dear," Helen answered as she patted her on the arm. "If you don't know, then I didn't do anything wrong. Now, there's my boarding call. Thank you again, and don't forget to invite me to the wedding."

"What wedding?" she asked, but the older woman was already walking away. Had she told Helen about George and Diane? Joanna shook her head, but couldn't remember. With a shrug she headed for the parking lot. She had a long night ahead of her, wondering how Nathan would react, or if he would.

Nathan settled into his seat, refusing the stewardess's offer of a cocktail. Shoving his carry-on bag and briefcase under the seat, he stared at the envelope in his hand. He was tempted not to open it, putting it off as he remembered the look on Joanna's face when she handed it to him. It had to have something to do with the baby, but what?

"You won't know until you open it, fool," he muttered, heedless of the passengers moving passed him in the aisle. He took a pen out of his inside pocket, and slit open the top of the envelope.

The legal looking document sent a chill down his spine, but it was rapidly replaced by the intense heat that suffused his body as he read the two pages. A red haze seemed to pass over his eyes, and when it cleared a second later, he was amazed to discover the paper crumpled in his hand.

The sudden jerk of the plane moving away from the gate brought him out of his daze. Though the stewardess was running through her safety routine, Nathan didn't pay attention. He read through the custody agreement twice. Damn if he was going to agree to any of it.

What was Joanna's motive for challenging him this way? She had to know that he'd be furious and refute everything that was in the document, that he'd demand— Nathan practically jumped out of his seat and ordered the plane to return to the gate, even as the front wheel of the jet lifted off the ground. He slumped back in his seat, his heartbeat erratic and his palms damp.

Joanna Trent had to be the most confusing woman he'd ever met, but that was why he loved her. And unless he missed his guess, she loved him, too. Tenderly folding the custody agreement, he tucked it in his coat pocket for safe keeping. Some women sent love letters, but his Joanna sent him legal papers.

He didn't think it was wishful thinking on his part. Those legal papers were a peace offering of sorts. She was giving him a way out, or a chance to meet her halfway. It took a lot of courage on her part, but how and when was he going to give her his answer? This wasn't something that could be handled in a phone call, it was much too important.

A bittersweet smile curved his lips, remembering Evan's advice as he signalled for the stewardess. Joanna was definitely something worth having in his life, and he'd willingly fight to win her, but it was going to take some skillful strategy from halfway across the country. The first priority when he got to Seattle was to see how soon he could get back to St. Louis.

"Why hasn't he called? Is he going to call?" Joanna murmured as she drove home from the hospital two days later. She'd been asking herself the same questions since she'd left Nathan at the airport. After spending the afternoon planning a whirlwind wedding with George and

Diane, she couldn't help but be a little melancholy. They were so sure of themselves and each other. Though she was happy for them, she also envied them a little.

As she approached the town park she could hear the sounds of children shouting and laughing through the open car window. She remembered running through the playground on a warm day like today without a care in the world. Impulsively she turned into the parking lot, and hesitated for a moment before shutting off the ignition.

The whole idea was crazy, but then nothing she'd done in the past few months seemed quite sane. Purposely she twisted the key and climbed out of the car before heading directly toward the swing set. Most of the children were heading home, but a few remained, giving the new arrival curious looks.

Before she could change her mind, she fell into the first swing and quickly pushed away from the ground to reach for the tree tops. She gave herself up to the freedom of the sky and rushing wind. Finally as her legs began to ache she let herself drift to a stand still, slightly out of breath. For a moment she sat very still as the exhilaration of soaring slowly wore off. Unfortunately, the problems she had escaped while in the air all came rushing back.

"Did you manage to blow away any of the cobwebs?" an amused voice asked from behind her, breaking through her thoughts.

"Brian," Joanna exclaimed, twisting around to face him, crossing the chains of the swing over her head. "You seem to be making a habit of sneaking up on me."

"Not really. I've been here for about ten minutes, watching you regress into childhood," he explained as he straddled the swing next to her.

"Just passing through?" she asked without looking at him as she continued to twist the swing, absorbed in watching the chain tangle above her.

"As a matter of fact, I was. I was jogging when I saw your car and came to investigate."

"Just a momentary fancy," she announced in a tone that was supposed to tell him to mind his own business.

"Who are you kidding, you or me?" he accused gently. "I remember this used to be your favorite trick when the problems of the world weighed too heavily on your shoulders. Uncle Brian can recall the time you broke up with Stevie DeAngelinus in the seventh grade. We spent three hours on this same swing set." Joanna didn't bother to comment on his reminiscences. "I thought my arms would fall off from pushing you, but you kept yelling, 'Higher, Brian, higher.' "

"You never were any good at pushing swings," she argued, lifting her feet from the ground to let the tightly twisted chain untangle above her head, spinning her in a contained circle.

"I had an interesting phone call yesterday, about adding some rooms to a house I'm designing. The man wants to add a nursery, which was strange for a man who isn't married," he stated tonelessly after she stopped spinning.

"What!" Joanna couldn't believe she'd heard him correctly.

"Nathan had some new additions to the house," he said slowly, his eyes anxiously searching her face. "Besides the nursery, he wanted to expand the office space downstairs, enough room for two people I'd say."

"A nursery?" What did it mean, a nursery and a double-size office? She almost didn't want to speculate, but she couldn't keep from smiling. When she turned to Brian, she had to choke back a laugh at the scowl on his face. "Brian, you look like some grim Puritan."

"You're pregnant?" His face was comical, his eyes wide and his mouth hanging open.

"You didn't know? Surely, you guessed— Did you

think Nathan had a family stashed away some place? Or possibly another woman?" She couldn't contain her laughter. There hadn't been much to laugh about lately, and Brian turning into a moralist was hysterical.

"I guess I have to apologize to Nathan," he said evenly, rubbing the back of his neck as a rueful smile curved his lips.

"What did you do?" she asked suspiciously.

"I wasn't too pleasant about the changes. In fact, I told him I didn't know how soon I could work on the project; I had other priorities."

"Oh, not too bright. And to think Chris was able—" she broke off. It wouldn't do any good to let him know his wife already knew about her condition. Too late.

"Chris knew?"

She nodded her head and waited while he muttered under his breath about feminine conspiracies.

"I guess I shouldn't have been so surprised. Nathan talks about you constantly. Sometimes it's gotten downright boring," he stated, trying to regain some of his former dignity.

"Really?" For the first time that day she lost the listlessness that had started as Nathan walked down the airport concourse.

"Oh, Jo, sometimes you're so transparent. If I didn't already think you were in love with the guy, that look would have given you away."

"There are times you can be too perceptive, but not too often."

"Cute. I'll admit that first meeting in Nassau must have been damn near explosive, due the effect it seems to have had on both of you."

Joanna didn't answer as she felt a flush rise from her neck. She'd been weak enough to admit to her feelings, but there were still some things that were private. She cherished those magic nights in the tropics and wouldn't share them with anyone, but Nathan.

"Uh huh! Chris said you wouldn't utter a word, and Nathan's like a clam. I innocently made a comment about what a coincidence it was you were both in Nassau at the same time."

"That's nice to know, but it doesn't help my current problem. Nathan and I have barely spoken in the last week and a half," she admitted, having the grace to look chagrined over the matter as she explained how it happened.

"Whoops. Not too bright, kid. However, I think you're worrying too much about the matter. He has added a few touches to the house to accommodate a family."

"We'll see," she answered, not wanting to start hoping too soon, "but sitting here while it's getting dark isn't going to help anyone."

"Very true," he returned, jumping to his feet. "However, you aren't going to escape so easily. I'm taking you home for dinner, or else you'll mope around your apartment all night."

"Not really, Brian, I'm a big girl now. I can take care of myself."

"Yes, I know you've grown up," he shot back with a leer and Groucho Marx eyebrows, "but I'm not a big boy yet. Chris says I'm not allowed out after dark, so I have an ulterior motive. I need you to drive me home, then she won't yell at me for being out late."

"Brian Judson, you're a fool." She laughed and linked her arm through his. "Come on, I'll protect you from your horrible wife. And as a reward for my recent therapy, I'll tell you something about George and Diane that Chris doesn't know yet. I'm amazed that she managed to keep the news of the baby a secret. That's impressive."

* * *

The phone began ringing as Joanna fit the key into the lock late the next evening as she returned from Diane's impromptu bridal shower. No one would be calling this late unless it was important, she thought frantically. The bell was still ringing as she yanked the receiver off the hook. But she couldn't quite catch her breath, a combination of running, astonishment, and excitement at the identity of her caller.

"It can't be you, you're in Washington," she exclaimed with nonsensical logic and dropped into the nearest chair as her knees gave out.

"And why not?" Nathan demanded indignantly. "I can dial a phone as well as the next man. What's wrong with saying hello, like everyone else? That's the normal greeting."

"Hello. Where are you?" she asked, still confused by his affable tone. Damn, he finally called after three days, he wasn't angry, and she was babbling.

"You certainly have an unorthodox method of talking long distance."

"I'm only functioning on one cylinder. I was just coming in the door when the phone started ringing." She shook her head to clear it. Maybe this was a dream, formed by her hopeful imagination. That was it. She was safely in bed, sound asleep and when she woke in the morning, this would be a fuzzy memory, like all of her other dreams of Nathan.

"What did you say?" she demanded, suddenly realizing he was talking again.

"I said the exercise was probably good for you and the baby."

"What exercise?"

"The run to the phone, remember? Your retention isn't too good. Have you been drinking?"

"Certainly not, but from your sparkling wit, I guess

you have," she returned, realizing the conversation much too peculiar for a dream, it had to be real.

"Joanna, are you still there?"

"Yes, Nathan, do you know what time it is?"

"Certainly," he said confidently, then after a slight pause stated, "It's quarter past ten."

"Maybe in Seattle, it's—"

"Skyhomish."

"What?"

"Not in Seattle, I'm in Skyhomish," he informed her with great patience, "that's where the work camp is."

"That's so nice to know, but it's still twelve fifteen in Kirkwood, Missouri, not the prime phoning hours."

"Not necessarily," he countered. "There isn't much else to do once the sun goes down here, except sit around and swap lies and exchange—"

"Liquor recipes?" she supplied with satisfaction.

"I haven't had too much to drink," he asserted quickly. "I had two beers, just enough to relax a little."

"If you relax much more you'll fall off that mountain you're on in Skyhomish," she answered, emphasizing the final word. "It must be the altitude then."

"Now, let's not get nasty, this is supposed to be a nice, friendly call."

"Is that what this is all about? Doesn't that make for an expensive pastime?" She wasn't sure why he called, but she was enjoying herself. The nonsensical discussion reminded her of the days they'd spent in Nassau, happy, relaxed, and carefree.

"Of course not, the rates change at eleven," he stated patiently, sounding amused again. "I do have to watch my budget, you know. There's going to be some unexpected expenses in my family soon."

"Don't tell me you planned this out ahead of time?"

"Well, actually, it didn't occur to me until about ten minutes ago."

"For heaven's sakes, why?"

"I was lonely, and I wanted to talk to you."

His reply had taken her completely by surprise. Every day she'd worried over his reaction to her demands. Now he was calling to talk nonsense, making only the slightest mention of the baby.

"Hey!"

"There's no need to shout, I'm still here."

"I thought you might have gone to sleep on me again."

"No, although it wouldn't be too amazing if I did," she told him in exasperation. The man was impossible, but she loved him anyway. "Did it ever occur to you during this brain storm, that I might be in bed?"

"Now that certainly conjures up a fantastic image," he murmured suggestively. "Why weren't you?"

"I was at a bridal shower for Diane. She's going to marry my brother in a few days."

"Lucky George. Maybe I should break my leg to get a little of that tender loving care he was bragging about when I visited him in the hospital."

"Somehow I can't see you as a helpless invalid." She barely managed to finish as a yawn overtook her in the middle of the sentence.

"What was that?"

"A yawn."

"I guess you want your beauty sleep, though you don't really need it."

"I do have to get up early tomorrow," she admitted, not wanting to break the connection. "Remember I have to work for a living?"

"I remember that."

"But I have a feeling you won't remember any of this

tomorrow," she stated with a chuckle at his earnest remark.

"Will, too," he answered firmly. "I suppose I should say goodnight."

"Goodnight, Nathan. I'm sure you'll have a good night's sleep tonight."

"Pleasant dreams, sweet nymph. I don't want any smudges under your gorgeous eyes when I see you again."

"Nathan, wait—"

It was useless, the only sound was the hum of the dial tone. She still didn't hang up, but sat staring at the receiver in her hand. Why had he called, even if he was slightly drunk? She was positive he wouldn't remember this tomorrow, but she would. In fact, she would undoubtedly lie awake half the night going over every word, still unable to make any sense of it. Whatever the reason, it had gotten lost as they talked.

She smiled at his foolishness as she hung up the phone and headed for the bedroom. He was usually so dignified and unconsciously arrogant. If he did remember tonight's call, would he admit it?

" 'Lo," Joanna's drowsy voice answered the phone after eight rings.

"You said you'd be awake this time, sweetheart. Last night you were barely coherent," Nathan said with an indulgent chuckle as she moaned in his ear. She'd told him the previous night that she was quickly becoming a midday person, incoherent anytime before noon and after six o'clock in the evening.

Leaning back in his chair and propping his feet on the desk, he complimented himself on the success of his phone campaign. The first call had been an impulse, a way to make contact to test Joanna's frame of mind. He'd purposely talked about nonsensical things, warily working his way through the conversation. By the end of the conversation, he knew she'd given him the custody agreement to open communication.

The second night he'd done the same, and Joanna didn't press him. Occasionally one of them would mention the baby, but never become too detailed.

"I thought you'd call earlier. Remember I'm sleeping for two now." Joanna's voice was a little stronger, but still husky with sleep.

He could tell she was sitting up from the rustling of the sheets, and almost groaned at the enticing picture that formed in his mind. Clearing his throat, he asked, "Are you taking your vitamins and getting plenty of iron?"

"Yes, Dr. Hartford," she replied primly.

"So, how are the wedding plans going?" he asked, shifting to safer ground quickly.

"I've decided that everyone should elope or live in sin, to save their relatives' sanity. Of course, everyone doesn't have George for a brother," Joanna explained, but her laughing tone told Nathan that she was enjoying herself. "He has help because Diane's dragging me from one store to another, looking for the perfect dress. Meanwhile, George is champing at the bit to get out of the hospital."

"I can sympathize with him. Is he going to make it in time for the wedding?"

"I think it'll be a photo finish," she answered, her words slightly muffled.

"Was that a yawn?" Nathan asked, dropping his feet to the floor. He could stay on the phone all night, but he knew Joanna needed her sleep. "I'd better let you go. Bubba needs sleep."

"I can't believe you're calling this baby, Bubba," Joanna complained as she had last night when he'd started it, though he thought he detected laughter in her voice.

"It makes sense. We don't know whether it's a boy or

a girl,'' he said reasonably. ''Bubba is a nice generic name. Brian agrees with me.''

''Brian's an idiot, but I'm glad he's speaking to you again.''

''Yeah, he told me he'd stopped polishing his shotgun. But now that we're friends again, he's bugging me about a starting date on the house.''

''What did you tell him?''

''I gave him a definite maybe for three weeks from now,'' he told her, holding his breath for her answer.

''You won't be home before then?''

Nathan grinned at the anxiety he heard. ''I'll be home sooner than that,'' he assured her, looking at the plane ticket laying on the desk, ''but I'll be in and out of town for a few weeks.''

''I miss you.''

He closed his eyes to savor the moment. ''I miss you, too. Now get some sleep, sweet nymph. I want you to be rested up when I get home.''

''Too bad we can't run away to a tropical island, and forget business and everything else in the world,'' Joanna said with a sigh.

''Sounds like a great idea to me, the temperature's been dropping here, and there isn't a beach or a palm tree in sight. I'd much rather see you in that yellow bikini than Mike Osaka in his overalls.''

''Hold that thought, love. Goodnight.''

''Goodnight, sweet nymph,'' Nathan replied, slowly hanging up the phone. He picked up the plane ticket and smiled. ''I'll see you sooner than you think, my love.''

TWELVE

"Excuse me, is this the Collins-Barringer party?" inquired a business-like voice from the doorway at the end of the waiting room. "The judge is ready for you now."

The wedding was a quiet, intimate affair. No one but the wedding party could guess it had been planned in less than a week. The bride and groom were suddenly very quiet and somewhat shy as the judge began the ceremony. Diane stood as straight as her diminutive size would allow, radiant in her pale green suit. As she made her responses in a barely audible voice, she cast demure glances at George from under the wide brim of her straw hat.

The groom didn't seem to be in any better shape. Bent forward slightly, resting his weight on his crutches, he attempted to appear in control. However, his true feelings became apparent when he had to swallow rapidly several times before forming the necessary words.

Joanna watched the couple torn between a sudden rush of feelings for the two people she dearly loved, and amused sympathy at her brother's endeavor to appear calm. He still tried to maintain his composure, but ruined the effect once more by running unsteady fingers up and down the lapels of his gray suit. He quickly recovered from the unfamiliar situation when he kissed the bride enthusiastically, nearly knocking her hat off.

When Diane tossed her the bouquet, Joanna sighed and looked up to meet Evan Hartford's amused gaze. Answering his wink with a smile, she took his proferred arm to follow the newlyweds to the elevator. "You're not worried about our little plan are you?"

"Of course, I am. I don't know why I let you talk me into it; Nathan isn't going to like it. I shouldn't be going anywhere," she answered, knowing that Evan would disagree. He was responsible for her sudden holiday. They'd had lunch the day before, and Evan *accidentally* told her that Nathan was flying into St. Louis on Friday afternoon. Impulsively, egged on by Evan and Diane, she'd made arrangements that would put them on neutral ground for their reunion. "What if we're wrong?"

"Nathan didn't have the family ring shipped to St. Louis, because he admires fine jewelry, my dear. This way you can have a few uninterrupted days to straighten out your problems," he said, making everything seem so reasonable as the elevator doors opened on the ground floor of the courthouse. "Now, if we don't get to the airport, George and Diane won't make their flight to Arizona, and you will be fretting over nothing."

She allowed him to lead her outside to the car. George and Diane were oblivious to the entire world while they snuggled in the back seat. Joanna couldn't sit still, despite Evan's assurances. Though Nathan alluded to seeing her soon during their late night conversations, he hadn't told her he was coming home.

Part of her was nervous that he'd be angry over what she was going to do, but deep inside she was excited. As the airport came in sight, she decided it was too late to turn back. Besides, Nathan would enjoy it, once he found her.

* * *

Joanna walked slowly down the planked walkway to the beach that was fairly deserted due the overcast weather. In her present mood she was glad she wouldn't have to cope with small talk. Evan had been wrong, or Nathan would have been here by now.

This was the first time she'd left her room since she arrived last night. Once she'd settled in her room she fell asleep with surprising ease after ordering a sandwich from room service.

Kicking listlessly at the sand, she began to wish that she'd stayed home, or that she'd picked a different hotel. Before she could stop herself, she focused on the float that bobbed innocently in the cove. That was where it all began, she thought with a bittersweet smile.

"If you haven't been the damnedest woman to locate."

He was here, or was she imagining it? She was tempted not to look, but couldn't stand the suspense. Here he was, a little rumpled and, if she read his glare correctly, more than a little out of sorts. Unsure of what to say, she took an involuntary step backward, then another.

"Joanna, we're going to play this my way now," he said and clamped a hand around her wrist. "I've been chasing you since yesterday afternoon. If you try to fight me on this, I'll probably strangle you just to relieve the tension."

It wasn't the most romantic speech she'd ever heard, but he was here. She wouldn't quibble, she decided philosophically. There wasn't time for another thought as he pulled her toward him, and the world tilted crazily as he tossed her over his shoulder like a sack of potatoes.

Too stunned to believe this was happening, she didn't utter a word as he strolled purposefully back toward the hotel. Her voice returned as they approached the front entrance to the hotel. Some of the guests eyed them with open curiosity, a few not bothering to hide their amusement.

"Nathan, for heaven's sakes, put me down," she hissed, wondering why she bothered to whisper. The guests probably wouldn't be amazed if she started singing *Yellow Bird*.

"Not on your life," he answered under his breath as he continued through the lobby. "We're going upstairs for a nice, private talk. One I'd planned to have in St. Louis yesterday."

"Private?" Now she was intrigued. "What was wrong with the beach? There wasn't a soul within miles."

"It's about as private as a fish bowl with every window in the hotel facing the beach. There was also too much running space," he said decisively. "I want you contained for our little discussion. I had enough when I was following your trail yesterday."

"Watch your head," he announced as he stepped into the elevator. She wasn't rash enough to say another word. The rapid rise and fall of his chest against her legs told her he wasn't in the mood for a debate. She remained mute during the short walk down the hallway to his room.

Once he unlocked the door, he didn't hesitate. Joanna saw a confused blur of colors and furniture legs as he walked across the room. She focused for a moment on a long strip of blue and grey striped material that fell to the floor. It was Nathan's tie. His belt followed seconds later, just as he walked into another room.

"What are you doing?"

He didn't answer as he came to a complete stop. Joanna took the opportunity to get her bearings. They were in a tastefully decorated bedroom, similar to Nathan's suite on their previous visit. The main decor was white with pastel accents. Her inspection was interrupted by the sound of jingling coins against wood. His shoulder beneath her hips rolled strangely.

"Damn it, Nathan Hartford, will you tell me what's going on."

"I'm taking off my watch so it won't get wet," he said cryptically, and she gave him a pithy answer. "Don't swear, Joanna, it doesn't suit you."

"I sure in hell will swear, if I damn well please," she snapped back, her patience running on empty. The blood was rushing to her head, and her arms ached from trying to push herself upright against his back. "And I will continue to swear until you tell me—"

A smart smack on her bottom effectively cut off her words. Nathan didn't say another word as he began walking again. Watching him shrug one shoulder out of his suit jacket and shirt, she decided to retaliate as a matter of principle.

Only the lower half of his body was available for her retribution and that suited her just fine. A malevolent grin curved her lips as she decided her revenge. Her fingers and thumb grasped as much of his buttocks as possible, before she pinched him. His yelp of pain was a very satisfying reward.

"Now will you tell me?" she demanded as he entered yet another room—white, gold flecked tiles replacing beige grass-paper wall coverings. Then the world tilted again as he lifted her off his shoulder. However, he didn't release her. She glimpsed a huge sunken tub filled with shimmering bubbles as she dangled helplessly above the floor. His right arm held her securely to his side as he pulled off the left sleeve of his jacket and shirt with his teeth.

"Would it be too much to ask why you're taking off your clothes?" she inquired sweetly, hoping a change of tactics would work. Though she found his current activity interesting, she wanted some answers, especially since his mouth had slanted into a smile.

"I haven't done anything but shave in the men's room of the Atlanta airport since leaving Seattle at the crack of dawn yesterday morning. So, I'm going to take a bath," he stated in a clear, concise tone as he pulled down the zipper of his trousers. He didn't even blink as the garment slid to the floor, and he stepped out of them. His only show of emotion was a gleam in his darkening eyes as he pushed off his shoes and pulled off his socks with his dexterous feet. "Since you're the reason I had to catch three puddle jumpers to reach Atlanta, only to sleep on a chair in the VIP lounge," he stopped for a minute to set her on her feet, "you're going to join me."

"Now, wait just a minute—" She didn't have a chance to finish before Nathan gave her a gentle push backward. Seconds later she was submerged in the bubbly, pine scented waters. Gasping and sputtering she came up for air. Her mind was working quickly, but the first clear image erased every thought from her mind as she wiped sodden hair out of her eyes—Nathan's anxious gaze.

"Evan was supposed to have a plane ticket ready for you," she said breathlessly, trying not to let his almost nude body distract her.

Nathan gave a short bark of laughter, then removed his last remnant of clothing. "My uncle has a perverse sense of humor," he explained as he stepped into the tub next to her. "If there was a ticket for me, he conveniently forgot to tell me as part of the Hartford work ethic. But do we really have to talk about my relatives right now?"

"Did, did you have something else in mind?" she managed through a sudden obstruction in her throat as he moved steadily toward her.

"Yes, I do," he replied conversationally as he worked at the fastening of her bikini top. "You might as well get used to this," he continued when he finished and his hands moved to her hips. He dipped his head to nuzzle her neck as his hands moved over her wet skin. "Now I have you exactly where I want you, I don't plan to let you out of arm's reach for at least the next twenty-four hours."

She was in complete agreement, raising her hands to stroke his shoulders lovingly. Since he was doing such an excellent job, she decided to let him handle the conversation.

"We're going to start all over again," he continued as his mouth trailed up her neck to her earlobe. She had difficulty concentrating as his hands closed over her aching breasts. "That day I approached you on the float, I didn't want any business complications. We'd get to know each other while we were here, then continue when I moved permanently to St. Louis. I didn't anticipate that you'd seduce me, then run off."

"I panicked a little. You were the first man in my life that mattered more than my work, my friends, or my family. At the time I didn't realize I was trying to hide from my own emotions, that I was afraid of becoming involved with you." She was amazed that it was so easy to tell Nathan her inner thoughts. Instead of hiding from what she felt, she was sharing it with the man she loved.

"Hush, sweetheart. The only thing you need to know right now is I love you," he ordered, making sure she complied by claiming her lips.

She trembled in delight as his questing tongue probed the inner warmth of her mouth. This was what she'd dreamed about and hoped for over the past week, but her practical nature was trying to break through. They still needed to talk. Their precarious relationship during the past month was a valuable lesson in the need for communication. The intoxicating movement of his hands and body were making it difficult to think, but when he rolled onto his back, she saw her chance.

Stroking loving hands up his wide chest to his shoulders, she bore down with all her weight as he gave an appreciative moan. Her smile of satisfaction quickly turned to a gasp of dismay when Nathan tightened his hold around her waist, pulling her underwater with him.

"What was that for?" he gasped as soon as they surfaced again.

"The fireman's carry from the beach, for starters," she answered with a chuckle, then cupped his damp face between her hands. "I wanted your undivided attention. I love you, Nathan Hartford."

"Thank God," he whispered fervently, not making a move to touch her or kiss her. "Give me five minutes, then we're going to have that talk about love and marriage and Bubba."

"All right, neutral corners," she agreed readily and scooted out of his way. Leaning back unselfconsciously to watch him, she stretched her arms along the side of the tub. She was still trying to believe he was here, and he loved her. His declaration hadn't really been necessary. No man went to the lengths he had in the last twenty-four hours, unless he was in love.

"What did you mean about the Hartford work ethic?" she asked dreamily, fascinated by the rippling movements of his back muscles. Maybe she should have offered to help.

"Evan is a guilty capitalist; he believes that a man should work hard for everything he has," Nathan explained, giving a snort of disgust before he went on. "He knew about George being your brother for almost a month, but he didn't bother to tell me. I think he was amused that I was jealous of George, and it made me strive harder for the prize—you."

"Oh, dear."

"Oh, you're sorry now," he accused in answer to her groan. Holding her gaze, he braced his hands against the side of the tub and leveled himself out of the water, walking toward her with a very determined smile that gave his mustache a devilish slant. Taking her outstretched hands, he pulled her to her feet. When her arms started to wrap around his neck, he stepped back and thrust a towel into her hands.

"First we dry off, then we talk. After that I'm open to suggestions."

"This is a very strange seduction," she muttered as she obeyed his instructions, wrapping her hair in the towel, then reaching for another to dry off.

Nathan plucked that towel from her a few minutes later before she could wrap it around her and swept her off her feet. "This has been a very strange courtship."

"I like being carried this way much better," she said, nestling her head into the crook of his shoulder.

"This is for romance; the other one was for practical transportation," he explained, dropping a kiss on the end of her nose. "The first night I did this, you thought I was going to drop you."

Before she could answer, he stopped beside the bed, the blue raw silk coverlet drawn back to disclose white satin sheets. A magnum of champagne was being chilled in a silver bucket with two beribboned glasses sitting next to it on the nightstand.

Joanna gave the romantic trappings a measured look before smiling up at Nathan. "I thought we were going to talk."

"We are, but I didn't take a vow of celibacy. And I didn't say we wouldn't be comfortable," he murmured before placing her gently on the sheets. She didn't argue as he quickly toweled her hair, and stretched out beside her when he was done. "If you'd been this cooperative in St. Louis, we could have cleared up this matter much sooner."

"Reached what point exactly?" she asked practically in a husky whisper, closing her eyes to savor the feathering movement of his hands gliding over her rib cage.

"To the point where we plan the wedding, I hope," he said softly, rubbing his cheek against her hair. "I made a few stops on the way here from the airport. One at the American representative and one for a marriage license at Government House. Between my English grandfather, and throwing my uncle the diplomat's name around, I now have a special license in my pocket."

"What?" Joanna sprang up, rubbing the top of her head where she'd clipped his chin during her precipitous move. "Are you proposing?"

"I'm demanding," he said simply, grinning at her bemused expression. "I need some permanence in this rather uneven relationship. I've had a lot of time to think up on the blessed mountain over the past week. You picked the setting, but I made sure we had the most extravagant surroundings, so you would know how much I want you. Trust me?"

"Yes, yes, yes," she responded happily, trailing kisses over his shoulder. When he ran his hands down her back, she arched against him and asked, "Do we really have to talk about this now?"

"I want everything to be straightened out before I get down to the pleasurable business of kissing you senseless."

"You are the most arrogant, overbearing man at times," she murmured against the solid wall of his chest.

"And you'd better love every arrogant centimeter," he demanded as he turned her firmly on her back, leaning over to kiss the tip of each breast. "Tell me, Joanna."

"I think I fell in love with you that first day on the float. I opened my eyes and there was this man in an indecent swim trunk who had an incredible smile." She clasped his head between her hands, looking directly into his dark eyes. "Deep inside I knew I wanted him for my very own and was amazed that he wanted me. But I got scared, everything was too perfect.

"Nathan, are you sure? It's not just the baby?" she asked, the last of her doubts surfacing in spite of his declaration.

"Love, desire, need, and want desperately," he told her without hesitation, punctuating each word with a fleeting kiss. "I knew the minute I saw you, and I couldn't put you out of my mind or heart, even when I was furious. The baby is a bonus, and maybe something of a test for us. We made it through a rocky courtship, so the marriage should get off to a good start."

"Nathan Hartford, I do love you," was all she could manage. She had a driving need to prove her love. With gentle pressure she pushed him onto his side, then his back. His smile of approval gave her the incentive to continue, her lips tasting the flat surface of his nipples. She remembered the night at the cabin when they'd made love in front of the fire, and she gradually moved lower.

His stomach muscles tensed as she explored the recess of his navel and her soft hands kneaded his lean hips. His gasp of pleasure as her warm mouth enclosed his engorged flesh spurred her on. Minutes later she murmured in protest as his fingers tangled in her hair, and he gently raised her head. Her protest was, however, silenced by the smoldering onyx of his eyes as he positioned her above him.

She took him into her sheath as their lips met in a kiss of promise. Slowly she matched his movements, savoring the sweet connection of their bodies. As his warm hands closed over her swollen breasts, she threw back her head and was unable to contain her moan of appreciation. Gradually she took them toward the summit of fulfillment, until he could no longer stand the pleasant torture of her seductive movements.

Deftly he turned her beneath him, trapping her objection with his moist lips. Their tongues entwined in heated desire as his thrusting hardness started their ascent to release. Holding her restless body firmly against his, Nathan prolonged the erotic agony. Joanna began to tremble in completion, crying out as he quickly followed.

He settled her passion satiated body against his side, and lay tenderly stroking the damp hair at her temples. She smiled, contentedly returning his caress, running her fingers down his cheek to rest on the soft bristles of his mustache.

"What's funny?" he asked lazily when she chuckled suddenly.

"I told Chris she should demand that Brian grow a mustache," she answered, her voice still husky in the aftermath of pleasure. "She was going to try. He's so susceptible when she's pregnant."

"I know the feeling."

"Nathan, I'm sorry I didn't have the courage to tell you about the baby sooner. It was all mixed up in being afraid of loving you, and there were a few red herrings along the way."

"You mean like finding out I'd been playing games when we first met. It was a harmless deception," he said with a heavy sigh, "but it certainly backfired. Evan would say it served me right for trying to take a short cut."

"Everything sort of escalated beyond our control," she murmured, letting her fingers explore the fascinating plane of his hair-roughened chest.

"I'd say we're even, and I have mine in writing." He paused for a minute as Joanna had the grace to flinch. "I actually considered high-jacking an airplane after I read that little gem you devised. Luckily, I realized what you were trying to do before I did anything drastic.''

"I'm sorry, but I didn't see any other way to open communication. Of course, I couldn't anticipate that you'd be thousands of miles away,'' Joanna stated to justify her actions. She wasn't all that contrite since her plan had worked. ''Besides you punished me for that one by not calling for two days, and then talking absolute nonsense when you did.''

"That was the only way I could think to handle the situation long distance. I was also still playing it safe, testing your frame of mind.'' He slipped his fingers under her chin to tilt her face upward. ''I wanted to know if you trusted me, and as Evan said, I needed to struggle a little to win the prize.''

"We both won the prize. I trust you with my love and my future,'' she told him earnestly, stroking his roughened cheek with her palm. ''I want to be a part of life, not just an observer. We have a fantastic future ahead of us.''

"You and me and Bubba,'' he pledged, his eyes gleaming with amusement as he captured her hand and placed a kiss in the palm.

"I might be persuaded to let you call our poor, defenseless child that silly nickname,'' Joanna told him, giving him a smile of invitation as she moved her lower body against his.

"That's an offer I can't refuse,'' he murmured and bent his head to the swell of her breast. They both surrendered to the passion that quickly flared to life.

EPILOGUE

"Isn't it time to put Bubba to bed yet?" Nathan asked in an offhand tone from where he paced in front of the fireplace. He stopped for a minute with his hands clasped behind his back.

"Nathan, you promised to stop that when the baby was born," Joanna exclaimed without looking up from the six week old infant in her arms. The baby didn't seem to mind the nickname, much more interested in suckling a bottle. "Bubba isn't even appropriate for a girl. Her name is Kate."

"Don't mind your Daddy, sweetheart, he's been a little bad tempered lately," she told her dark-haired daughter. Kate opened her blue eyes, blinking in answer as she continued to drain the formula from her bottle. "Nathan, what's wrong with you? You've been like a caged animal since we got here this afternoon. I thought you wanted to come down to the cabin to relax."

"Relaxing wasn't exactly what I had in mind," he explained, resuming his pacing again.

"Well, what else would—" Joanna broke off as he gave her a baleful look. For a moment she was disconcerted by her own naïvéte. After eight months of marriage—especially marriage to Nathan—she should have known better. She curved her lips into an inviting smile, and asked, "Would your plans have anything to do with my doctor's appointment this morning?"

"Now what makes you say that?" he asked innocently as he walked across the room to sit down next to her on the couch. Leaning against her shoulder, he began twisting a lock of her hair around his finger.

"Probably because you kept the motor running while I was in Dr. Jessup's office this morning," Joanna answered, snuggling her shoulder closer to his chest. "Tell me more."

"First, I think our daughter needs to get some beauty sleep," he said, his gray eyes intently watching Kate fist her eyes and scrunch up her tiny face. "See, she knows when her parents need time alone."

Joanna removed the empty bottle from Kate's rosy mouth, and thrust it at Nathan. She maneuvered her daughter into a sitting position and rubbed her back until she felt a small hiccup. Giving her husband a sidelong look from beneath her lashes, she asked, "Why don't you put her in the playpen, while I slip into something more comfortable."

Nathan jumped to his feet, then reached down for the baby. He held her close to his chest as he pulled Joanna to her feet. Joanna moved willingly into his one-armed embrace. He kissed the top of her head. "Happy?"

"Extremely," she answered with a sigh, looking down at her daughter's round face. They'd gotten off to a rocky start, actually doing everything backward, but they'd survived the storm.

She'd been foolish to turn her back on life. Loving Nathan and Kate was the most glorious experience of her life. And their bond of love grew stronger every day. She would explain that to Kate as she grew older. Her daughter was going to meet life head on, and not hold back.

"What was that about quality time?" she asked, turning her face up to meet her husband's dark gaze. He accepted her invitation, his lips meeting hers in a promise of a lifetime of love.